Two Steps Back

Back

a novel

Britni Danielle

www.BritniDanielle.com

Two Steps Back. -- 1st ed.
ISBN 978-1499582727

To everyone who ever encouraged this dream:
thank you.

"Love does not begin and end the way we seem to think it does. Love is a battle, love is a war; love is a growing up."

–JAMES BALDWIN

1

"What do you mean you're pregnant?" Mrs. Baldwin glared at her daughter like Jaylah had declared she was swapping Jesus for Satan. "Please tell me this is some kind of joke."

Jaylah wished it were a trick. She wished she could yell, "*Sike,*" just as terror crept across her mother's flawless face causing it to crinkle in delight as the pair dissolved into a cacophony of giggles. Unfortunately, it wasn't a prank. Jaylah had fled to London to find herself and had come back a damn statistic.

I guess what they say is true, she thought, *freedom isn't ever really free.* Jaylah had paid dearly in weeks of exhaustion and morning sickness for a pregnancy she wasn't even sure she wanted to keep.

"How did this happen?" Mrs. Baldwin asked, incredulous. Jaylah shot her mother a look. *Are you serious?*

Her mother's eyes bore into her demanding an answer, and Jaylah threw her hands up in surrender.

"It just happened."

Jaylah didn't want to argue with her mother, she was no match for Sarah anyway, especially now when she just wanted to crawl into bed and sleep for two days straight.

"So while you were traipsing around England being footloose and fancy free you couldn't bother to protect yourself?"

All Jaylah could muster was a meager shrug. "We used condoms, mother. But apparently they aren't foolproof."

Mrs. Baldwin paced around the well-appointed living room, stopping at the granite mantle to mumble to herself like she was attempting to calm down. Jaylah knew her mother was pissed and trying her hardest not to go off on her only child, but she didn't care. Not anymore. After years of living up to her parents' near-perfect expectations, Jaylah had finally found her own groove in London. Unfortunately, it came with a baby and boyfriend who lied about his wife.

"And who is this guy? Please tell me you know who my grandchild's father is."

Jaylah rolled her eyes so hard she thought they'd shoot out of her skull. She may have gone and gotten herself knocked up, but she wasn't showing up on Maury Povich's stage anytime soon.

"Of course I know who he is."

"Good." Mrs. Baldwin mother tapped a finger to her chin and Jaylah knew the wheels of her mind were whirling with a plan. "Well, let's see. You'll move home, have the baby, and your father and I will help you out while you look for another job and get back on your feet."

"I have a job at *Glamour*, remember?"

"They'll let you keep writing from here? Wonderful!"

Jaylah closed her eyes and rubbed her temples; she was starting to get annoyed. She'd allowed her parents free-reign to plan her life before, but at 28 and pregnant, the rules had changed. This time, she couldn't just sit back and be bossed.

"No mom, I'll be going back to London in a few weeks. Besides, I don't even know what I want to do about the baby yet."

Mrs. Baldwin spun on her heels and glowered at her daughter. "What did you just say?"

Jaylah cleared her throat and instantly felt like her t-shirt was a straight jacket squeezing all the air out of her lungs. She had never defied her parents, had never gone against their wishes, even in the most benign situations. But this was different; she wasn't about to allow herself to be guilted into having a baby—not by Johnny, or Jourdan, or even her mother.

"I'm not sure I'm having this baby," she said, finding her voice.

Mrs. Baldwin's eyes went wide. "Is that what that man is telling you to do? Kill my grandchild?"

"No, he actually wants me to have it."

Mrs. Baldwin blew out a puff of pint-up air. "At least one of you has some sense. I raised you better than this, Jaylah. You get pregnant, you deal with the consequences."

"This isn't some afterschool special, mom. And I'm not a dopy teenager who got knocked up after the prom. I'm 28, and for the first time *ever* I'm enjoying my life. I'm not sure I'm ready to trade it all in for a baby."

Jaylah's mother opened her mouth to speak, but quickly closed it. She crossed the room to the wet bar and poured herself a quarter of wine. She took a long, lingering sip, and then swished the dark liquid around in the crystal glass.

"Being a mother is the greatest job you'll ever have. You will cherish every minute of it, even when your baby breaks your heart." She drained the wine in two large gulps, then turned to her daughter. "I trust you'll do the right thing, Jay Jay."

Jaylah watched her mother sashay out of the room, and let her words wash over her.

Do the right thing.

Jaylah wondered how four simple words could add up to such a conundrum. If she knew what the right thing was she would have made up her mind to do it before she left London, before getting on the plane, before telling Johnny to *please, please, please* stop pressing her for an answer about their future.

If she knew what the right thing was she'd gladly do it, but that just wasn't the case.

Jaylah retreated to her childhood bedroom and curled up on the bed. The walls were still her favorite shade of purple, the ceiling was still peppered with the glow-in-the-dark stars she'd put in the fourth grade, and her TLC and Fugees posters still clung to the walls. Artifacts from her old self stared Jaylah in the face, but it felt like she was looking at someone else's life.

Everything was so damn simple then, she thought. *I wish I could hit the rewind button and go back because this shit right here is HARD.*

Jaylah needed time—preferably years—to sort this all out, but with a child growing inside her, she knew she'd have to make up her mind—fast.

2

The alarm rang, startling Jaylah awake. She fumbled through the darkness to grab the phone before it screeched any louder, but by the time she located it the thing was beep-beep-beeping so vociferously she thought it would wake up the whole house. Jaylah swiped the kill switch, and then blinked rapidly to adjust her eyes to the darkness and make out the time: 11 p.m.

She did the math in her head, adding eight hours to account for the difference in time zones before calling him. She hadn't talked to Johnny since she'd gotten back to Los Angeles two days ago. All she'd sent was a text message saying she made it safely and would speak to him soon. They'd traded voicemails, but between readjusting to Pacific Standard Time, and her propensity to slip into a pregnancy-induced coma, they had failed to connect.

The phone rang a handful of times before going to voicemail. Johnny's accented baritone kissed her ear and caused her to smile in spite of herself. Even though their relationship hovered somewhere between totally committed and don't ever call me again, his voice still made her knees wobble—just a little.

Jaylah left yet another polite message before dialing her best friend.

"Jaaaaaaaaaylaaaaaaah," Jourdan sang into the phone instead of saying hello. "You know I'm upset with you. I take it you've made it safely and didn't land on some deserted island in the Pacific."

Jaylah rolled her eyes and chuckled. "We didn't fly over the Pacific, silly. Anyway, I can't manage to stay awake long enough to actually call anyone. Apparently this child is not only eating all of my food, but zapping my energy too."

"How is my little niece or nephew?"

"I told you not to get too attached. I still don't know if I'm having it."

"Whatever. We both know you are."

Jaylah sat up in bed and glanced down at her stomach. "I'm not convinced, but you can add my mother to the list of those lobbying for me to keep it," Jaylah let out a heavy sigh. "I told her."

"See! You're totally having this baby! How'd she take it?"

"Well, let's see. First she basically called me a whore and asked if I knew who the father was, then she informed me I'm moving home and she and my father will help me raise the baby."

"So it went well, did it?" Jourdan chortled.

"Ehh, she didn't curse me out or slap me, so I guess so."

"Great! But Jay, tell your mum she can't have you back. It's my turn. You're coming back to London in a few weeks, yeah?"

"Yup, with or without a baby."

"Definitely with. Look, I need to get my ass in gear if I'm going to catch the Tube and make it to work on time. I went out last night, and lets just say I'm still a little tipsy."

"Sounds like fun. I could use a drink right about now."

"Don't worry, I had enough for the both of us. I'll call you later, yeah?"

"Okay. Love you, J."

"Love you too, Jay."

Fully awake, Jaylah sat in bed trying to think of something other than food. At the rate she was going, she thought the baby would push her body over the edge from curvaceous to gigantic before her second trimester. But after minutes of listening to her stomach grumble, Jaylah got up and wandered into the kitchen for a snack.

Resistance was futile; score one for the kid.

She rummaged through the refrigerator and cupboards looking for something that wouldn't come roaring back up her throat soon after eating it, and settled on a glass of flat 7-Up and a handful of graham crackers. As she munched on the sweet treats, her mind wandered to Johnny. Despite telling him that she needed time to figure things out, before she left London he'd doted on her like an ecstatic husband happily awaiting the birth of his first child.

And he was; only he wasn't *her* husband.

Jaylah grabbed her phone and decided to try him again, hopeful that a couple dozen minutes would garner a different response than last time. She checked the time, it was just after 7:30 a.m. in London, and from the weeks they'd spent cohabiting in her flat she knew he should be wrapped in a towel shaving the hairs that dared to sprout up on his smooth face.

The phone rang and Jaylah twirled a piece of hair around her finger trying to organize what she would say. She ached to be curled up next to Johnny, his arms draped around her just so, but that would only complicate things, and make it harder for her to think straight about her own future, let alone theirs.

"Jaylah?" Johnny sighed into the phone like he'd been holding his breath too long.

"Hey. Getting ready for work?"

"You know it. Just putting my shirt on. I've got to hurry, I have a meeting this morning." He dropped his voice to a sexy whisper. "You okay? I miss you, babes."

A ripple traveled straight up Jaylah's thigh to her belly. She knew it wasn't the baby; it was him, always him. He could turn her on with the twist of a simple phrase.

"I'm fine. Just been really, really tired. I think I've been asleep since I got here."

"Get all the rest you need. I wish I could be there to help you move. Please don't over exert yourself, okay?"

She brushed his concern aside. "I've got it covered, my parents are helping me and I've hired a couple of movers."

"Good. I was thinking, maybe I should fly out there one weekend so we can tell your parents about—"

"They already know," Jaylah cut him off. "I was exhausted and throwing up like a drunk and my mother kept hounding me to go see a doctor. So I just came out with it."

"How'd they take it?"

"Well, my mother thinks you're the only one with any sense."

"Me? How so?"

"She launched into her plan—move home so she and my father can swoop into action and help me with the baby."

"That's not even an option, right?"

"Not at all. I told her I wasn't even sure I was having this baby, and—"

"Jaylah, please don't—"

"What?" She crossed her arms defiantly even though she was in the kitchen alone. "I'm not. And nobody is going to rush me on this."

Johnny let out a long, exasperated breath. "Fine, but you know what I want. I want you and our baby."

"Anyway." Jaylah refused to acknowledge his statement. "She said you were the only one with any sense because you want me to have it. She said I need to 'accept the consequences,' as if having a baby is akin to being grounded. Can you believe her?"

Johnny was silent. Jaylah knew he agreed with her mother, knew he wanted her to have this baby, their baby. But she still wasn't convinced.

Jaylah heard a woman's voice in the background. *Is that the TV? Johnny hates listening to the news in the morning,* she thought. But the woman's voice grew louder.

"Who is that?" Jaylah pressed her ear to the receiver and realized the voice was calling Johnny's name, asking him, "Coffee or tea."

"Who is what?" he said, seemingly unaware she could hear the voice.

"That woman, in the background. I thought you were at home."

"I am," he swallowed audibly, "it's Fiona."

"Fiona, *your wife?* I thought she was in Scotland?"

"She was until yesterday—"

"How convenient. I leave and she slips right back in. Is this how it's going to go, Johnny? Tag, she's it?"

"Calm down, Jaylah. It's not even like that. Nothing happened, or will happen."

Jaylah smacked her teeth and paced around the kitchen. *Fucking Fiona,* she thought to herself, *Johnny thinks he's slick.*

"Look, you have a good time with your wife. Bye Johnny," she said, but paused to hear his response. Could he explain why his soon-to-be-ex-wife was making him coffee despite the fact they'd decided to divorce?

Or had they?

The thought shot through her brain. *He could be lying about that as well.*

"Jaylah, please. I didn't even know she was coming back. She showed up last night and—"

"And you couldn't tell her to leave? Are you even getting divorced, or what? Is this some sort of elaborate scheme to keep us both? I know your African ass isn't trying to turn me into a second wife!"

As soon as the words crossed her lips Jaylah regretted hurling such an ugly stereotype, but every nerve in her body felt like a balled up fist ready to strike.

Jaylah was crazy about Johnny. She longed to be with him—despite his wife, despite the baby—and it terrified her. If she was willing to overlook his lie, what else would she eventually turn a blind eye to?

Wasn't the saying, "How you got him, is how you'll lose him"?

Even though she'd just left the comfort of his chest days before and was carrying his child, would Jaylah eventually end up losing him to another woman, or worse, his wife?

"Johnny, how do I know this whole thing isn't just some temporary affair? How do I know you won't magically get back together if she wants to work it out? I mean, is that why she's back?"

She could picture him rubbing his eyes like he always did when she flew into one of her hormone-induced fits. "It's not. And we're not working anything out. This is her home too, Jaylah."

"Whatever," she spat. "When is she leaving?"

"She says she's not."

"Okay, when are *you* moving then?"

"I don't know. My townhouse has two bedrooms. I was thinking, I can just stay in the guestroom until I find something more permanent."

Jaylah looked at her phone. *Is he for real?*

"Absolutely not."

"Jaylah, apartments take time to find and—"

"Ab-so-lute-ly not!" she repeated, this time stretching the words out for emphasis. "If you stay there I swear this whole thing is over. I'm not about to try to figure out what to do about this baby *and* worry about you sleeping with your wife. I refuse!"

"I'm not sleeping with her, Jaylah. I just need some time to sort out a place to stay. You already know the divorce is happening. You went with me to the solicitor."

She sucked her teeth again. "What does that have to do with the price of tea in China, Johnny?"

"I'm sorry, what?"

"Look, move out of there by the end of the week or you can forget about us. Period."

"Just like that?" he asked in disbelief.

"Just like that."

Jaylah hung up the phone without saying goodbye or even uttering another word. Her mind was made up. Johnny could not, under any circumstance, live with his wife. She understood this probably made her sound unreasonable and totally insecure. But Jaylah was not about to be played for a fool by the only man she'd ever truly loved.

The stakes were just too high.

3

"Wake up sleepyhead," Mrs. Baldwin said as she tapped on Jaylah's bedroom door. She could hear her mother's nails rapping against the wood, but refused to move. After their conversation last night she was in no mood to hear another lecture, so Jaylah reverted back to her high school self and pretended to be a dead body.

When Mrs. Baldwin noticed her polite wakeup call wasn't garnering any results she walked to the window and yanked back the blackout curtains Jaylah begged her to install in when she was in the tenth grade.

"It's after 1 p.m., Jay Jay, time to get up!"

"Ugh," Jaylah grunted, pulling the striped duvet over her head. "I'm still jet lagged, mom. Do you know what the time difference is between here and London?"

"Eight hours. Now get up, you have an appointment."

"An appointment? The movers aren't coming till Saturday. That gives me two days to catch up on sleep."

"Later," she said moving to Jaylah's bedside and pulling back the cover. "Get dressed, we're going to see Dr. Lawson."

"For what?"

Mrs. Baldwin raised an eyebrow; Jaylah already knew.

This damn baby is already cramping my style.

"Can't you reschedule, mom? I'm exhausted."

"Do you even know how far along you are?"

Jaylah felt groggy and irritated, her mother was on a mission and would not be stopped, no matter what Jaylah said.

"A few weeks, maybe a month." She shrugged. *What difference does it make?* she wanted to ask her mother, *I'm probably not even having it anyway.*

"Exactly. You have no clue," her mother patted the cover. "Up and at 'em. We're leaving in a half hour. And Jaylah?" Mrs. Baldwin ran her hands over her daughter's unruly hair, "please do something about this."

Jaylah watched her mother leave then stared at her starry ceiling. She flirted with the idea of skipping the shower and grabbing fifteen more minutes of shuteye, but seeing a doctor without properly bathing was just straight up wrong, so she pulled herself out of bed and schlepped to the bathroom down the hall.

Jaylah turned on the hot water and stepped into it before allowing it to cool. Penance for her stupidity. It stung her flesh, but she did not move, just stood there as it burned her back. Three minutes passed before she eased on the cold water, turning her shower tepid to match her tears.

Jaylah did not want to see Dr. Lawson, her personal physician since she was a teen. She didn't want to let yet another person down and have them look at her like she'd thrown away her life. Yes, she was grown enough to not give a damn about anyone's opinion, but she did, especially those who loved her.

"Keep it together, Jay. No need to fall apart now," she said aloud, continuing a ritual she'd started in childhood. While other kids created best friends out of thin air, Jaylah talked to herself. Whenever she had a problem, was feeling down, or conflicted about something she'd ask herself for advice. It was strange, but Jaylah had to admit, she rarely led herself wrong.

This time was different, however. This time she had no clue what to do, but she was running out of room to decide.

"Everything will be fine, right?"

"Right," she answered. "Even when it ain't. It's still okay."

Jaylah dried her face, jumped out of the shower, and scurried back to her bedroom to get dressed. She picked out a red animal print dress and slathered shea butter on her chest, arms, and elbows, then paused when she got to her belly.

"What the fuck am I going to do about you, huh?" she asked the blob growing inside her. "Your timing couldn't be any worse. You know that, right?"

She paused, waiting for the blob to answer the question (or apologize), but nothing happened.

"Figures," she grunted. "I bet if I had a sandwich you'd speak up."

Jaylah stifled a giggle and rubbed more Shea Butter across her stomach hoping to stave off any stretch marks even thinking about scaring her skin. If only figuring out what to do was just as simple.

⊛⊗⊜

Dr. Lawson's office was as bright and annoying as Jaylah remembered. The walls were painted fire engine red and preschool blue as if she were a pediatrician instead of a general practitioner who catered to teens and 20-somethings who were too afraid, or too stubborn, to make the switch to a "grown up" doctor. Jaylah had been seeing Dr. Lawson since she was 14 when Dr. Johns, her pediatrician, suggested she might feel more comfortable visiting the teen lounge. Her mother scoffed at the recommendation, telling Dr. Johns in a huff, "But those girls are having sex! I don't want a doctor who hands out condoms and tells Jay Jay, 'Good luck!'"

Mrs. Baldwin had nothing to worry about, of course. Jaylah didn't dare have sex, too scared she'd get knocked up and publically shamed. She'd seen how the pregnant girls in her church were paraded in front of the congregation to repent for their sins and Jaylah vowed she would never ever make that walk alone. Jaylah didn't even *talk* about sex until she got to college, 3,000 miles away from her mother's all-knowing ears. But after meeting Emile, a Haitian-born Brooklynite with soft lips and wandering hands, her freshman year at NYU, all of her mother's advice to keep her legs closed flew out the window.

Jaylah stared at the giant fish tank in the corner of the room and tried to will herself to disappear. She did not want to be there. Not in the doctor's office, not even in L.A. She let her mind drift back to her favorite spot in London, the café at the Tate Modern. The first time she ambled to the second floor eatery looking to grab a quick snack before seeing the rest of the galleries at the museum, she was not prepared for what she would see.

A wall of glass overlooking the south bank of the River Thames, St Paul's Cathedral dominating the sky, and the Millennium Bridge stretching across the water. Jaylah stared out of the windows, transfixed. It was as if she was gazing at a postcard come to life, and in that moment she knew she'd actually made it to London—its gray sky threatening rain, boats trudging to and fro, and Jaylah standing in the middle of it all.

As she sat in Dr. Lawson's office waiting for the nurse to call her name, she longed to be back on the South Bank, waiting for her breath to be taken away again. She was tired of thinking about the baby or how her life was in complete upheaval. She wanted to be back in her flat, or at the Tate, or dancing with Jourdan, or tucked away in Johnny's arms.

Jaylah sighed and tried to push him to the farthest corner of her mind. She couldn't think about him right now, not when she had her mother breathing down her neck about the baby. Jaylah felt ganged up on, everyone wanting—no, demanding—her to have it as if raising a child was as easy as deciding on a new hairstyle.

Having a baby would mean deferring to someone else's needs—again. Hadn't she done that enough? Hadn't she always been the perfect daughter, sensible friend, good employee?

Moving to London had been her stab at finally reclaiming herself. After a lifetime of being upright, levelheaded Jaylah she did something crazy. And it worked. She'd met a friend who was more like a sister, snagged a job writing for *Glamour*, fell in love, and for the first time in her entire life felt completely comfortable in her own skin.

And now this, Jaylah thought, sucking her teeth so loud her mother turned to look at her. *Everything was going so well and I couldn't even enjoy it for a year. Three months, that's all I got, then bam!* She shook her head as an unruly chuckle rolled through her body. *What the fuck am I gonna do now?* The question banged around in her head demanding to be answered.

"Baldwin! Jaylah Baldwin," the nurse called, dragging her out of her thoughts.

Mrs. Baldwin stood first, grabbed her things and headed to the door. Jaylah eyed her mother and suppressed a laugh.

She really thinks I'm still a child.

Jaylah watched as Mrs. Baldwin stepped past the nurse to wait for her. Jaylah could have protested, could have told her mother to have a seat in the waiting room, but why bother? She'd just have to repeat whatever Dr. Lawson said, verbatim, so why not just cut out the middle man?

The nurse led Jaylah and her mother down a small, neat hallway. The walls were lined with pictures of smiling patients, some holding babies, some merely staring into the camera with grins slathered on their faces. Jaylah grew increasingly annoyed as she moved through the corridor and felt like slapping every single ounce of happiness out of the Polaroid people.

This was not a happy time. Jaylah was confused and exhausted and ready for this whole distraction to be done. She wanted to ask God for a do-over. Jaylah wished she could go back to whenever she and Johnny had conceived this child and do something differently—insist he wear two condoms, tell him to pull out, get a double dose of the Plan B pill.

Unfortunately, there were no take-backs. Jaylah couldn't rewind the clock; she was stuck in the present, and would have to deal with this before everything spun too far out of control.

"Here you are," the nurse said directing Jaylah and her mother to a tiny room. "Get undressed and put this on. Dr. Lawson will be with you in a minute."

"Thank you," Jaylah said, then turned her attention to her mother, "Do you mind?"

"Oh please, Jay Jay. It's not like I haven't seen you naked before."

Mrs. Baldwin took a seat in the corner and fished through her purse. Jaylah glared at her mother, rolled her eyes and began undressing. She decided to conserve her waning energy for more important matters than a pointless argument.

"I hope Dr. Lawson doesn't take too long," Mrs. Baldwin said while Jaylah slipped into the gown. She ignored her mother, sat on the examination table, and tried to get comfortable while paper crunched beneath her.

Dr. Lawson knocked on the door quickly before poking her head inside. "Ready for me?"

"Yes, we're ready," Mrs. Baldwin answered before Jaylah had a chance to open her mouth.

"Great! Jaylah, so good to see you. How's everything?"

"Pretty good, Dr. Lawson. Well, except I'm pregnant," she half-laughed, half-shrugged.

"I see. How far along are you?"

"Well—"

"She doesn't know. That's why we're here," Mrs. Baldwin cut in.

Dr. Lawson raised an eyebrow. After seeing Jaylah for the last fourteen years she knew just how overbearing Mrs. Baldwin could be.

"Okay, well, let's try to get to the bottom of it today," she said, patting Jaylah's hand. "Mrs. Baldwin, would you mind waiting for us out front? These rooms are so small and I'll probably need to bring in the ultrasound machine."

"Uh, sure, sure," Mrs. Baldwin stammered.

"Thank you. I'll call you back in before we wrap-up." Dr. Lawson winked at Jaylah.

Mrs. Baldwin gave the pair a tight-lipped smile. "See you in a bit."

Jaylah stifled a laughed and waved at her mother as she walked out the door. "Thank you. She still thinks I'm a kid."

"Old habits die hard. Now, what's this about you being pregnant?"

"I know," Jaylah threw up her hands.

"Was it planned? You're 28, correct? These *are* your prime childbearing years."

"No, not at all. We even used protection and every-thing."

"I see. So, are you happy about this or..."

"Definitely or," Jaylah huffed.

"Gotcha. When was your last period?"

"The third week in July," Jaylah said, remembering how she'd been so excited about her new city, and then caught up in the news that Johnny was married that she didn't even realize she'd missed her cycle. "I noticed I was late in August and took a pregnancy test."

"Okay, let's see what's going on here. Assume the position," Dr. Lawson said, smiling.

Jaylah put her legs in the cold, metal stirrups and tried to relax. She hated getting pelvic exams, didn't like anyone probing around in her ladyparts unless they were trying to get her off, but Dr. Lawson made the situation slightly more bearable. She would walk Jaylah through the process and explain exactly what she was about to do, even though they'd both been down this road several times before.

"I'm just going to insert the speculum, so I can do the pap test first, okay?"

"Umm hmm," Jaylah responded, willing her mind to think about other things, happier things.

"Now I'm just going to use the little spatula to obtain a cell sample from your cervix to make sure every-thing is alright. You may feel a slight discomfort."

Jaylah winced and resisted the urge to snap her legs shut. She closed her eyes and counted backward from 100. By the time she got to 70, Dr. Lawson was done. "Everything looks fine. I'll have the results of your pap in a few weeks. Now, let's see if we can figure out how far along you are. Be right back."

Dr. Lawson left the room, but quickly returned with an ultrasound machine that looked like a compact computer workstation. She motioned for Jaylah to open her gown, and then smoothed a thick coat of cold jelly on her torso.

"We may not be able to see or hear anything, especially if you're less than six weeks along, but hopefully we'll get lucky," Dr. Lawson said.

Jaylah stared at the ceiling, unsure she wanted to see the blob in action. She'd been trying not to think of the mass as a little person growing inside her lest she be clubbed over the head by attachment.

But she was curious.

As Dr. Lawson ran the probe over her belly Jaylah stared at the screen, straining to catch a glimpse of the blob swimming inside her. She thought about ringing Johnny on Skype so he could also see the blob fluttering about. It would surely make his day, and after their argument about his wife's reappearance and Jaylah's ultimatum, they needed something to soothe the anger and hurt feelings.

But she resisted, calling him would only further complicate things.

Jaylah refocused her attention on the florescent lights above her head and pretended to be 5,000 miles away from the exam room that felt like the walls were closing in and she was going to suffocate. In her mind, Jaylah was back on the Tube, zipping through the tunnel on her way to go shopping in Oxford Circus, wandering around Camden, or meeting Jourdan for drinks at the Satay Bar.

As she fell further down the rabbit hole of her imagination, Jaylah pictured herself back in her flat in Highbury typing away on her column while Johnny tries to lure her away from the computer with kisses and the promise of Jamaican take out. After finally giving in, the pair cackle like they've known each other for years, not months, and their playful flirting turns into steamy love making on her couch.

"Hmm..." Dr. Lawson said, cutting Jaylah's daydream short. "I think we may have something. Hear that?"

Jaylah closed her eyes and focused on the faint drumming coming from the machine. Dr. Lawson turned up the volume and a team of horses galloped out of the speakers and straight to Jaylah's heart.

"Is that..." she asked, breathless.

"Yup, that's the heartbeat! Now, let's see if I can actually get a look at the fetus."

"Oh my God," she mumbled, gobsmacked. "That's really it?"

"Yeah, it sounds very healthy, too."

Jaylah didn't know what to think or feel or say. The horses felt like they were hurtling through her body rendering her nervous and mute. After weeks of trying not to think of the blob as a person, but rather an unfortunate inconvenience, she was completely caught off guard by this moment. *That's my baby? That's my baby? That's my baby?* Jaylah turned the question over in her brain again and again hoping to find an answer.

While Dr. Lawson moved the probe around Jaylah's belly trying to catch a glimpse of the fetus, Jaylah grabbed her phone and dialed Johnny. She did not know what she would say, or why she was even calling him given their recent blowout. But she needed to share this moment and it was only fitting that it would be with him.

"Jaylah?" he answered with a sigh, "Look, I'm still at the office and don't want to argue."

She put him on speaker. "Can you hear it?"

"Hear what?" he asked, sounding annoyed. "It's late and I need to get out of—"

She moved the phone closer to the machine. "Listen."

The team of horses picked up their pace, seemingly spurred on by their voices. After a few seconds of drumming, she heard Johnny's voice catch in his throat.

"Can you hear it?"

"Yes, yes, my God, yes," he said. "It's so fast."

"And strong," Dr. Lawson said. "And look at that. There it is."

"What? What?" Johnny asked, slightly panicked. "Everything okay?"

"Everything's fine," Dr. Lawson and Jaylah answered in unison.

"See that? That's the fetus," Dr. Lawson said, pointing to the blob on the screen.

"It's so tiny," Jaylah whispered.

"Yeah, about the size of a kidney bean. Less than an inch. Judging from the size of the fetus, and the date of your last period, you're about eight weeks along."

"That far?" Jaylah gasped. "That's two months!"

"It's still very early. A typical pregnancy lasts for about 40 weeks, so you have quite a lot of time to go if you decide the fetus to carry to term. But you need to make up your mind quickly, okay?"

Jaylah nodded. "Okay."

"Great. You can get dressed. Do you want me to send your mom back in?"

Jaylah shook her head.

Dr. Lawson chuckled. "I don't blame you."

She left the room and closed the door. Jaylah stared at her phone and got lost in the deep crevices of her mind.

"Thank you," Johnny said, bringing her back to the moment.

"What?"

"Thank you for letting me hear that. It was," his voice cracked, "beautiful."

"What are we going to do, Johnny?" She was asking herself just as much as him.

"You're going to come home, we're going to get married, and we're going to raise our baby," he said firmly.

"Married? You're already married."

"Yes, but not for long."

"We shouldn't rush into anything, Johnny. The timing couldn't be worse. We've only been together a few months, I just got a job, and—"

"Things don't always go according to plan, Jaylah. But we can make it work."

"How do you know? It didn't work with your wife."

"Can you stop saying that? This is totally different."

"How? You guys got married because she was pregnant. How is this any different?"

"Because I want to be with you, Jaylah," he said, exhaustion creeping into his voice. "Can't you see I'm crazy about you? I want to build a life with you, and I *want* to marry you."

"Because I'm pregnant."

"Because I love you."

Jaylah rubbed her temples and let Johnny's words hang in the air. She knew he loved her, knew that he meant well, but was that enough? Could love sustain them through a pregnancy, his divorce, and whatever else that would come their way?

She appreciated his sense of duty, but she wasn't convinced that they were the exception—the couple who could overcome a troubled start and crazy drama to live happily ever after.

"Are you still there?" he asked.

"Yes, I'm here. I don't know what to do, Johnny. And I'm tired of trying to figure it out."

"I know, babes, I know. But things will work out, I promise. Just..." he hesitated, "please don't kill our baby, Jaylah. Please. Not after today."

Jaylah put her clothes on in silence and tried the process the last 15 minutes of her life. She walked into the doctor's office intent on ridding herself of the blob, but now it was a baby, *her baby.*

"Did you hear what I said, Jaylah? Please don't kill our baby. We can make this work, I know it."

She wasn't sure they could overcome the odds, but everything within her prayed Johnny was right.

4

Jaylah stood in the middle of her living room and surveyed her former life. The walls she meant to re-paint three years ago still lacked the cheerful colors she'd picked out; functional, yet nondescript, furniture dotted the room; and pictures of her family clung to the walls. The whole scene looked appropriate, but im-personal—much like Jaylah's old life.

Six months ago she sleepwalked through the days, going from her cubical at the *L.A. Weekly* to her as-signments and back to her couch. Jaylah threw herself into work, never refusing to cover an album release party, concert, or film screening no matter how much she thought she was better suited for weightier assignments, or didn't want to attend. The result? She grew to hate her job, and her personal life was damn near nonexistent, consisting of very few friends, men she slept with on occasion, and her parents—always her parents—stepping in to fill the gaps.

Getting fired from the *L.A. Weekly* felt like a huge slap in the face. After five years of writing about topics she could give a rat's ass about, Jaylah felt like she'd paid her dues and should have had free reign to cover things she was actually passionate about—the social implications of pop culture, politics, race. Her time at the paper afforded her a comfortable lifestyle and the façade of success, but it didn't make her happy. Instead, she felt like she was drowning.

Six months ago Jaylah did not, could not, know that getting fired would be the best thing that ever happened to her, but it had. She became a woman unleashed, no longer burdened by a job she couldn't stand, a city she felt she'd out grown, and a mother who showed love by controlling her every move.

Losing her job, leaving L.A., and moving to London had been her chance at liberation. And she grabbed it and ran.

Jaylah gazed around the room trying to decide what would get boxed and shipped to London and what would be housed in her parents' garage. She picked up a vase her boss had given her for Christmas and marveled at just how ugly it was with its frosted glass and cobalt blue waves. She moved to put it in the box marked "storage," but quickly changed her mind. Instead, she went to the balcony, checked to make sure no one was around, and hurled it to the ground.

A surprising sense of satisfaction spread through her as shards of glass scattered across the driveway. Old Jaylah would have wrapped the vase in paper and stored it away for safe keeping despite hating it. But this new woman, unbound by her former life, wanted it gone. She returned to the living room looking for something else to smash to bits, but realized her things were too well kept to destroy. In that moment, she devised a new plan.

Jaylah moved through her apartment snapping pictures on her phone and thinking about how much she could get for the items she no longer wanted. There was no need to pay thousands of dollars to ship things to London and no need to hire movers to haul her stuff to her parents' garage when she knew she would never need them again.

New Jaylah didn't want anything from Old Jaylah's life except for her vast collection of books, the jewelry box and diamond earrings her parents had given her when she turned 13, and her pictures. Everything else could go up for sale.

Before her old, sensible self could come barging back in, Jaylah called the movers and canceled her appointment, then cracked open her laptop and began placing Craigslist ads for her things.

I'll donate whatever doesn't sell, she thought, already feeling a thousand pounds lighter because of her decision to get rid of the remnants of her former life.

When she was done cataloging and writing ads, Jaylah surveyed her apartment with fresh eyes. For once she didn't feel instantly depressed by her solemn, unimaginative space; she felt hopeful.

Her rebirth had actually happened; it wasn't a fluke. Her move to London hadn't been some sort of apparition; it was real. And she was determined to make it work, no matter what.

5

"What time will the movers be at your apartment on Saturday?" Mrs. Baldwin asked when Jaylah returned home after spending the balance of the day listing her things for sale.

"Oh, they're not coming. I changed my mind."

"About moving? Thank goodness! I was hoping you'd stay here instead of running back to London like some teenager."

Jaylah took a deep breath to calm her nerves. She knew her mother would not take kindly to her new plan, but she didn't care.

"I'm going back to London, mom. I just decided to sell my things instead of storing them. I don't really need them anyway."

"Sell your things?" Mrs. Baldwin huffed. "I thought you were keeping them here? You don't even know if this whole London thing is permanent."

"It is," Jaylah said, keeping her voice even.

"And what happens if you want to move back, or if you need to come home?"

"Then I'll come home," she said, staring directly at her mother. "Daddy likes to park in the garage anyway. My stuff wouldn't be doing anything but taking up space. And I don't need it."

Mrs. Baldwin sucked her teeth and looked to her husband for backup. He was reading a book in the corner of the room, trying to stay out of his wife and daughter's disagreement—as usual.

"Jay Jay, I know you think going back to London is a good idea, but your father and I were talking about it, and we think you should stay here. I mean, who's going to help you with the baby?"

Who says there'll be a damn baby?! Jaylah wanted to yell, but decided against it.

"Mom, I know you and dad want the best for me, but I'm a grown up, okay? I have a job there. I have friends. I'll be fine." She softened her tone. "And you're always welcome to come visit."

"*Friends,*" Mrs. Baldwin spat, "don't help you raise babies."

"*If* I decide to have this baby I will have all the help I need, mom."

"If?" Mrs. Baldwin asked, glaring at her daughter. "You're still talking about if?"

"Yes, if."

Jaylah's mother opened her mouth to respond, but decided against it. Instead, she called on her husband before leaving. "Joe, please talk some sense into your daughter."

Mr. Baldwin put his book down and crossed the room to sit on the couch with Jaylah. His salt-and-pepper hair was cut close to his scalp, and his almond-shaped eyes, the ones he'd given Jaylah, crinkled as he smiled.

"You know we just want the best for you, baby girl," he said, patting her on the leg.

"I know, daddy. But mom still treats me like a child. You should have seen her carrying on at the doctor's office like I was some unfortunate teen mom."

"I can imagine," he chuckled, "but this is important stuff. It's not quite happening how we wanted, you know. Your mom and I always thought we'd be walking you down the aisle before you had a baby, but things happen. We just want to make sure you're alright."

"I am, daddy. I'm just not letting anyone pressure me into motherhood."

"You got that from me," he smiled. "I can be kinda stubborn, too."

Jaylah stared into her father's face and saw her own. Their high cheekbones from her Coushatta great-grandmother, their umber skin that glowed red in the summer, their long, fluid frames. She was definitely her father's child, and for that, she was thankful.

"Daddy, I know you and mom want me to have this baby, but I feel like my life is just now starting to get on track. Having a baby would totally interrupt it."

"I understand, baby girl," he said comforting her with his words.

"How can you? You and mom did it the right way," Jaylah said using air quotes.

Her father hesitated, gazing into his daughter's face before speaking. "I know it seems like that, but things are never simple. Now, your mama and me were always sweet on each other. We grew up together and lived on the same street, but didn't start dating until we both ended up at Howard."

"I know. I've heard this story a million times. You saw each other at a party and have been inseparable ever since."

"Yeah, well, sorta. But baby, you were a bit of a surprise."

"A surprise? You guys got married in your senior year and I was born after graduation. How surprising is that? Mom always says she wanted to graduate with her B.A. and her M.R.S."

Mr. Baldwin chuckled, shaking his head. "Yes, we were planning on getting married, just not so soon.

But your mother found out she was pregnant with you, and—"

"You got married because mom was pregnant?!"

Jaylah couldn't imagine her mother getting knocked up before walking down the aisle. All of the talks about sex her mom had doled out over the years. All of the warnings and the lectures about waiting until she was married before giving away "her precious gift" came flooding back into Jaylah's brain. If she had ever stopped to do the math—her parents wedding anniversary falling in November, her birthday in June—she would have known something was up. But she didn't. She never had a reason to question her mother's words.

"Baby girl, we got married because we loved each other. You just moved up the timeline a bit."

Jaylah sat stunned. First Johnny had rushed into marrying his wife because she was carrying his child, now this. Was she just falling into some sort of fucked up family cycle—first comes unexpected pregnancy, then marriage?

"Were you scared, dad? Were you worried you were making a huge mistake by getting married because mom was pregnant?"

"Of course I was scared. But we loved each other and had been planning to get married anyway. I just didn't expect to be a dad so early. We wanted to be married for a few years, travel first, see the world. But it worked out," he said, giving Jaylah's hand a squeeze.

She replayed her life looking for signs her parents only stayed together for her sake. She rarely heard them argue, and they took vacations to Florida or Jamaica or down South every summer.

When she was little, Jaylah would love watching her parents dance to old Motown tunes in the middle of the living room. They'd look so happy, her dad doing his best two-step, and her mom twirling like a teenage girl. It had been good, right? They seemed to make the right choice.

"So…" Jaylah hesitated, "if you could do it all over again you wouldn't change anything?"

"Of course not. I love you and your mother. Being your dad is the best thing that ever happened to me, baby girl," he said as his eyes, Jaylah's eyes, slanted upward as he smiled. "I know you've got a lot to consider, and I'm here for you either way. But just know things will work out exactly the way they're supposed to—no matter what."

Mr. Baldwin kissed Jaylah on the forehead, then grabbed his book and headed down the hall. She found comfort in her father's words and hoped he was right.

"Things will work out exactly the way they're supposed to," she said aloud over and over again, hoping it was true.

6

The phone rang, causing Jaylah to awake suddenly. She blinked, adjusting her eyes to the burnt orange light filtering through her curtains and tried to figure out if it was morning or dusk. *What time is it?* Jaylah thought, as she rummaged through the covers and under her over-stuffed pillows for the phone. She cursed whoever it was who had the nerve to interrupt her sleep; it was such a scare commodity these days. Even though her belly hadn't exploded into a watermelon, she still couldn't seem to sleep through the night. Tossing and turning and getting up to pee had become commonplace these past few weeks as the blob—now baby—had taken over her body.

She located her mobile just in time for the caller to give up. Jaylah checked the time: 6:47 a.m., Saturday.

"Saturday? What happened to Friday night?" she asked herself, before remembering she'd decided to take a nap after struggling to finish an article the previous evening. Apparently, she had fallen into a coma.

This baby was not only wreaking havoc on her body, but it was also causing her to lose focus. Writing had once come easy; she would enjoy getting lost researching a topic, and then compiling her thoughts. But since the blob came to town she'd found it difficult to sit still, to think, to write, or to work.

Sitting in front of the computer now felt akin to torture, her mind getting stuck on *what the fuck am I going to do?* instead of the task at hand, her column. Hillary, her editor at *Glamour,* had been accommodating, allowing Jaylah to file articles while she returned to the States to get matters settled before moving back to London. But would she be as accepting of a pregnant writer who couldn't seem to keep two thoughts, let alone anything poignant, in her head at once?

Pregnant women have been working for centuries— running companies, writing books, teaching school. Surely Jaylah could pull it off, but she wasn't sure she even wanted to try.

"It's not fair," she whined to Jourdan during their last conversation. "My life was just starting to get fun. Now this!"

"Oh get over it, Jay. You're not the first woman to be up the duff. You'll survive."

"But I don't want to *survive*," she said, rolling her eyes. "I want an extraordinary life."

"And you can have that with a baby."

"Maybe, but do I have to have it right now? I mean, look at Oprah. Look how awesome her life is and she doesn't have kids."

"She has a billion dollars. She could have 80 kids and her life would still be amazing."

"Whatever. I read that she said if she had kids she wouldn't be who she is today. Can you imagine?"

"So you want to be Oprah?" Jourdan teased.

"Don't you?" Jaylah retorted. "But seriously, I just don't want to feel like I'm being held back, and babies hold you back."

"They can also give you wings, Jay."

Jaylah checked her missed call log—Johnny.

She lay in bed and waited for the drowsiness to subside before returning his call. They hadn't spoken since her doctor's appointment, the heartbeat interrupting her plans and confusing things even further.

He called four times since then, leaving messages and even sending an email, but she hadn't called him back, too unsure of what she would say.

I love you but maybe not the baby. I'm totally confused. I'm scared out of my mind. You better have moved out or else. I can't do this alone.

All of Jaylah's thoughts seemed so desperate, so weak, so opposite of who she was becoming.

She dialed Johnny's number and held her breath. Her stomach lurched when she heard his voice seep into her ear causing her to lose focus and get lost in her uncontrollable longing to be next to him.

"Hello Mr. Poku," she said, trying to keep her voice light.

"Hey. Did I wake you?"

"Of course." Jaylah snuggled further into her pillows, wrapping her arms around one of them like she would do to Johnny if he were there.

"Sorry, babes. I tried not to call too early. I took a chance. Why haven't you returned my calls?"

"I've been busy. I decided to sell my things instead of ship them to London, so I was handling that. And the time difference makes it hard to connect."

"Are you sure that's it?"

"What else would it be?" She wanted to add: *other than the fact that I have absolutely no clue what to say, and I'm sick of you pressing me for an answer about this baby?*

"I just feel like you're avoiding me."

"Why would I be avoiding you?"

"I don't know, which is why I'm asking. Maybe I'm just paranoid, babes. I miss you. I wish I could be there with you."

She rolled her eyes. "And why aren't you?"

"I wasn't invited."

True, Jaylah thought. She hadn't asked Johnny to come to L.A. with her, afraid he might just take her up on the offer. Can you imagine how her mother would react to her daughter's married boyfriend who had fathered her child? Chaos would certainly ensue.

"Well, consider yourself invited," she said.

"Seriously? I will get on a plane, Jay. Don't tempt me."

"I'll see you when you get here." Jaylah chuckled to keep from sounding too intense, but she *was* serious, at least partially. She wanted to see him in the worst way, even if she wouldn't admit it.

Johnny let out a rush of air. "I'm in a hotel, you know. I'm at the Hoxton and I hate it. I feel like I'm living in a box."

Jaylah smiled, pleased Johnny heeded her warning to move out of his house without putting up a fight or plying her with excuses. She made a mental note to call the hotel and ask them to ring his room—she had to be sure; she couldn't *just* rely on his word, could she? Not when he neglected to tell her about his wife until she was already in way too deep.

"Then you better find an apartment quickly."

"I wanted to talk to you about that. I was thinking that maybe I should hold off on finding a place until you get back. We can look for one together."

"I already have an apartment, Johnny."

"I know, babes, but it's not really big enough for three people."

"Three people?" Jaylah scrunched up her face.

"You, me, and the baby."

Jaylah sucked her teeth. "Johnny, don't start."

He ignored her protests. "We might even be able to buy a flat right there in Highbury Stadium. I spoke with an agent and they've got some open units. You like that neighborhood, yeah?"

"I do, but it's super expensive and I can't afford to buy anything right now. I *just* got a permanent job for Christ's sake. I can barely make the rent on my own flat."

"I'm not asking you to pay for anything, Jay, I can handle it," he said in the same tone superheroes use before striding into a burning building to rescues the screaming, but insanely beautiful, woman trapped on the top floor.

Jaylah wondered what letting Johnny rescue her would feel like. Would she have to give up her dreams in exchange for a comfortable life? Did she even want him to swoop in and save her from this mess (that he helped create) or did she want to flex her own muscles and save herself?

"Listen," he said, snapping her out of her thoughts, "just think about it, okay? I'm going into a tunnel. I'll call you back in a few, babes. Love you."

I love you too failed to escape her lips but Jaylah felt it spreading through her body like a gentle nudge pushing her to surrender. Six days—the amount of time it had taken her to become completely obsessed with the gorgeous Ghanaian man she met on the dance floor of the Mau Mau bar. Six nerve-wracking days, and a ride on the London Eye was all it took for her to fall—hard.

Five months had passed since the night Johnny entered her life, but it had felt like five years. Their relationship—so hurried, so intense, so anything unlike she'd ever experienced before—had resulted in an unexplainable bond that could only be described in clichés. Love at first sight. Soul mates. Better halves. Kismet.

Pick one.

What Jaylah felt for Johnny did not make any sense. But the day he showed up on her doorstep and found out she was carrying his child, she stopped trying to figure it all out.

Before Jaylah gave in to the tide of emotions she Googled the number for the Hoxton and rang the front desk—just in case.

"Hello, I'm calling for one of your guests, Mr. Jonathan Poku," she told the clerk. "P-O-K-U."

"Okay ma'am, give me a moment to check," the cheerful woman said. Jaylah listened as the woman's fingernails clicked rapidly on the other end of the line and she kicked herself for being one of *those* women. The needy, distrustful kind who filed away every bit of information their man ever told them so it could be verified later.

She didn't want to become one of those women, but Johnny had not given her much of a choice. She had to be sure he was telling her the truth. She had to be sure he wasn't trying to have his wife and Jaylah on the side.

She couldn't *just* take his word for it, right? Not now at least. Not with her whole life on the line, and not until she was sure that this thing was actually for real and not just a temporary blip, or an itch he needed to scratch before running home to Fiona.

Jaylah hated herself for becoming a stereotype—the snooping, suspicious woman—but she hated Johnny for planting these thoughts in her head in the first place. Although he'd been straight up with her since coming clean about his wife, she found it hard to believe everything he said without giving it careful consideration, or checking the story for holes.

Jaylah knew that she couldn't go on like this. She knew they were on a slippery slope that would end in checking Johnny's pockets, his phone, or breaking into his email to find evidence of lies. That was certainly not a life she imagined, or wanted, for herself but she had to be sure—at least for now.

"Ma'am?" The woman's voice was back on the line. "He's in room 528, I'll connect you straight away."

She let out an audible sigh; Jaylah didn't realize she had been holding her breath.

"Thank you."

7

"I'll be back, mom."

"Where are you going, sweetie? The Sampsons are in town and your daddy and I are having dinner with them. They haven't seen you since high school, why don't you tag along?"

"Not really in the mood for a reunion, but I'll let you know."

Jaylah hurried out the door and got into her car. She clutched the steering wheel and took three deep breaths, exhaling hard like she was in a yoga class before cranking up her Honda. It had been two weeks since she'd been back in L.A. holed up in her parents' spacious View Park home, and although it was roomy rio to not to see each other for long

Jaylah was beginning to feel like a

needed to break out or die.

.ıı her car trying to decide where to go, eve-
ɩything she could think of seemed *too* L.A. for her
taste. Though she was born in the City of Angeles,
Jaylah had always been a peculiar Angeleno who most
assumed had migrated to the city from the east coast.
She hated going to the beach, didn't care about celeb-
rities, and rolled her eyes every time she met someone
"in the business," which was always because, technical-
ly, so was she. After moving to New York for college
Jaylah preferred her winters brisk, her summers sticky
and unbearable, and relished the ability to ditch her
car and hop on a train to go anywhere she pleased. Los
Angeles was certainly her birthplace, but it had never
really felt like home.

Jaylah pulled out of the driveway and onto Angeles
Vista heading up the hill. She passed blocks and blocks
of stately homes, and a few McMansions, before spilling out onto Slauson, which was the thoroughfare that
connected the 'hood and "Black Beverly Hills," making
each more interesting in the process.

"Hmm, right or left?" Jaylah asked herself at the
stoplight. When she felt her stomach growling she decided to head west toward the ocean.

Jaylah snaked her way up Slauson until she came to
an onramp for the freeway. She merged onto the four-
lane beast and prepared to inch along for miles on end

but, to her surprise, traffic moved at brisk clip and she was in Santa Monica before she knew it.

Instead of grabbing a bite and walking along the Promenade with the rest of the tourists, Jaylah kept north on Highway 1, stealing glances at the water that crashed against the shore. Though she hated most of the beaches in L.A. she had always been drawn to the ocean and could gaze at it for hours on end, wondering what was going on below the waves.

At 10, Jaylah read a book about mythology and learned people once believed Poseidon was the God of the Sea. But having spent most of her summers gazing at the ocean she thought the Greeks had gotten it completely wrong. *How could a woman not rule the ocean?* she wondered. The water so perfectly mirrored how women actually are—calm on the surface until they're pushed too far, and a flurry of activity just beneath the skin.

Jaylah had always felt like the ocean—enticing those around her with soft edges, good grades, fine manners, and a reliable work ethic, while silently planning to smash them to bits and tear down the façade when the opportunity presented itself. The problem? The time never seemed to come.

After college she slipped right back into her role as dutiful daughter, brunching with her mother on weekends instead friends; throwing herself into work at the *L.A. Weekly* despite knowing she was too brilliant a writer to cover Twitter trends and indie bands; and allowing sometimey men to share her bed because she was too afraid to be alone and too unsure of herself to demand more.

Getting fired and moving to London had caused an earthquake in her sea, and Jaylah could feel a tsunami building that would send everyone scrambling for higher ground.

Jaylah saw a sign for El Matador State Beach and decided to stop. She pulled into the parking lot, paid the toll, deposited her car, and walked to the edge of the cliff overlooking the ocean. She stared out over the magnificent view, taking in the gigantic rocks jutting out of the sand and marveling at the translucent blue water that she thought was impossible in L.A. Jaylah took a moment to thank the Goddess of the Sea, then strode toward the hiking path that lead down to the shore.

When she got to the bottom of the hill, Jaylah ambled along the coastline and through a cave before coming upon a family of seals sunning themselves on the rocks. She watched as the mother gently groomed her pup, carefully nuzzling its slate-gray body with her whiskers while it lay on the jagged rocks. She looked on as an overeager photographer crept a little too close to the baby to snap a picture, and was startled by the mother's piercing bark telling the man to stay away.

She eyed the pair, transfixed by their bond and wondered if she could ever love the blob like that. Would her primal instincts kick in and push her to protect her baby at all costs if someone got too close? Could she put her child's needs above her own? Could she and Johnny really have a life together and raise a child?

In that moment, Jaylah finally realized what she wanted to do. Now, all she had to do was tell Johnny.

Jaylah pulled her phone out of her pocket and called him up. She didn't care that it was nearing midnight and he had to work in the morning; she had to speak to him *now*.

"How soon can you get here?" Jaylah asked the moment he answered the phone.

"What?" he stammered, "are you okay?"

She could hear the panic rising in his deep voice and it comforted her. Despite her doubts, despite her uncontrollable need to check and double check whatever he said, she knew that he loved her.

"I'm fine, Johnny. I'm at the beach and I was looking these seals, and—"

"Seals? I don't understand. What are you talking about?"

"I made up my mind, Johnny. I know what I want to do about the baby."

"Oh," he hesitated, "and what have you decided?"

"How soon can you get here? I want to tell you in person."

"Why can't you just tell me now?"

"Because," Jaylah said slightly annoyed. "Anyway, you said you would come. When can you get here?"

Johnny let out a deep sigh. "Saturday. I can probably be there Saturday."

"Okay. See you Saturday."

Jaylah hung up the phone before he could take back his promise to see her in two days. She knew she probably sounded crazy, but Jaylah had finally made up her mind about something that would affect their lives in one of the biggest ways imaginable. Telling him over the phone seemed to be wholly impersonal and inadequate, and well, she ached to see him.

Jaylah hiked back up the hill and asked the Goddess of the Sea for strength. She and Johnny were certainly going to need it.

8

"I'm headed to the airport, mom. I'll be back," Jaylah called over her shoulder without even thinking. She hadn't told her parents Johnny was flying into town because didn't feel like having a long, drawn out discussion about what kind of man he was or what his intentions were. Jaylah wasn't even sure she wanted tell them he was in L.A. at all.

"What's at the airport?" he mother asked, flipping through a magazine.

Jaylah considered making something up, but decided against it. "Johnny."

"Johnny? Is he one of your friends from college?"

"No, he's my..." Jaylah didn't quite know what to call him. Her soon-to-be-divorced boyfriend? Her baby's father? The first man she'd ever truly loved? Her obsession? "He's my boyfriend, mom. He flew in from London for the weekend."

Mrs. Baldwin put down her magazine and stared at her daughter. "And you're just now telling us?"

"We weren't sure he would be able to get a flight. It was kind of last minute and I wanted to wait until I knew for sure he'd be coming," Jaylah lied. It seemed better than saying, *I didn't want to tell you because I knew you'd make a big damn deal of it.*

"Oh." Mrs. Baldwin glanced at her watch, then looked at the ceiling and began murmuring under her breath. She appeared to be running a list through her head, her fingers keeping score. "Well, it would be hard to pull off a proper dinner in such a short time. I'd need to scrub this place down, go shopping, and start cooking, but it's already after one."

"That won't be necessary mom, he'll probably be jet lagged anyway. He's been flying all night."

"Okay then, tell Johnny we'll expect him for dinner tomorrow evening."

"Mom, that's really not necessary. This is his first trip to L.A., he'll only be here a few days, and—"

"And nothing. Your father and I need to meet this man. He *is* the father of your child, isn't he?" There it was again, the subtle, *you're a hussy* jab. Mrs. Baldwin glared at her daughter as if she had lost all sense of decorum.

"Of course, mother."

"Then we need to meet him and hear what his plans are. Jaylah, you're our only child. You expect us to sit back while you have a baby, *in London*, with a man we don't even know?"

Jaylah rolled her eyes, resisting was futile. "Fine mom, we'll see you on Sunday."

"You *are* coming home tonight, aren't you?" Mrs. Baldwin asked, cocking an accusatory eyebrow.

Jaylah hadn't planned on it. If the weekend unfolded the way she hoped, she would be snuggled up beside Johnny for the next two days. "I'll call you later."

❦

Jaylah stood in the baggage claim fiddling wit her hair. Since 9/11, people were no longer allowed to meet their loved ones at the gate as soon as they deplaned, instead they were forced to play a chaotic game of hide-and-seek amid hundreds of weary travelers scrambling to claim their bags.

She paced a narrow strip of the floor and eyed the escalator, growing increasingly annoyed each time a person descended the moving staircase that wasn't Johnny. A raucous colony of bats banged around in her stomach making her feel like she wanted to vomit, and she thought about running to the nearest restroom, but swallowed back the feeling.

Jaylah laughed at her nervousness, thought it silly she was carrying on like a schoolgirl who was hoping to catch a glimpse of her crush in the hallway between classes. Johnny had had this affect on her from the beginning—unsettling and enticing her all at once.

The crowd streaming into the baggage claim began to thin but there was still no sign of Johnny. She took out her phone and checked for missed calls, then texted him again: "WHERE ARE U???"

Ten minutes passed and there was still no answer; Jaylah was beginning to feel sick again. She plopped down on a bench that still allowed her to watch the escalator, and checked her phone.

"He said 3:30, right?" she asked herself, scrolling through her email to find his flight information.

"He better be on this plane," she said after confirming she was definitely on time. Then it happened again, the need to check his story overtook her. Jaylah looked up the number for Virgin Atlantic and waited patiently for a customer rep to confirm Johnny was a lying asshole—or not. She steeled herself for either one.

"Hi, I'm calling to see if a passenger boarded a flight. I'm waiting for him in the airport and he should have been here by now," Jaylah said, rambling to the agent. "His name is Jonathan Poku. P-O—"

"I'm sorry ma'am, we don't give out that type of information," the woman said.

"No, you don't understand. I'm not a stalker or anything, he's my boyfriend and I've been waiting for about an hour now, and—"

"I apologize ma'am, but we don't give that type of information."

"Well, can you at least tell me if he made it to Heathrow on time?"

"Ma'am—"

"Please? We haven't seen each other in weeks and I'm pregnant and I'm just stressing out about it. Sorry."

"It's ok ma'am," the woman said, softening her tone. "Let me see."

Jaylah's grip on her phone tightened and she could hear her heart beating in her ears. She braced herself for the worst.

"Ma'am? A passenger by the name of Jonathan E. Poku checked in at Heathrow at 18:37 GMT on Friday, but I cannot confirm if he boarded the plane."

"Thank you," Jaylah whispered. "Thank you."

She hung up and immediately felt silly. "Why would he send me his flight information if he wasn't going to show? Of course he's here. Of course," she reassured herself.

Jaylah watched a new rush of passengers flood the escalator and began to feel hopeful again. Her heart knocked around so hard she pressed a hand to her chest to get herself to calm down. She stood to her feet and walked toward to the crowd. *He has to be with them*, she thought as she searched the faces for her lover's.

But he wasn't there.

Forty more minutes passed and Jaylah sulked back to the bench, defeated and increasingly worried. She tried to push the negative thoughts out of her mind, but they kept creeping in. *He changed his mind. He's not coming. He doesn't want you; he wants Fiona. He's her husband, after all. You're just his whore.*

Jaylah shook her head to dislodge the thoughts in her brain. Tears began welling up, and she jammed the heel of her palms to her eyes to stop them from spilling over.

"Get it together, Jaylah," she commanded. "Stop acting like a fucking cliché!"

She counted backward from 100 to take her mind off crying, then decided to give Johnny a few more minutes before she left.

She checked her watch. "If you're not here in 10 minutes, Johnny, you're on your goddamn own.

Hunger crept through her body, gnawing at her insides, and for the first time Jaylah realized she hadn't eaten all day. She had been too nervous to eat, scared whatever she ingested would come rushing up her throat. Her plan was to pick Johnny up, have lunch, and get him settled into his hotel, but that had been nearly two hours ago and she was barely holding on.

Five minutes. She prepared herself for the worst and wondered what she would tell her parents about his sudden Houdini act. Her mother would certainly see Johnny's failure to materialize as yet another reason Jaylah needed to forget about London and stay in L.A., but that was off the table.

"No matter what happens, I'm going to do what's best for *me*," she told herself. She had spent the majority of her 28 years living for others—her parents, her friends, her job—she wouldn't add Johnny to the list.

"I love him like crazy, but I come first," she reminded herself, "I come *first*."

A fresh group of travelers descended the escalator and Jaylah gave them a passing glance. Time was up. She stood to stretch, grabbed her purse, and took one last look at the group before she headed toward the door. She massaged the back of her neck and walked through the sliding glass. When she stepped outside her phone buzzed.

"COMING DOWN NOW."

Johnny's message stopped her cold. Jaylah peered through the plate-glass windows and saw him— shoulders slumped, shirt rumpled, head swiveling back and forth, scanning the room. He didn't look like the self-assured man she fell in love with; he was a mess.

A minute ago she was pissed off and ready to leave, now she was moving through the crowd toward the escalator, a smile tugging at her heart.

Johnny saw her standing at the foot of the stairway and returned her smile. He jogged down the remainder of the steps, grabbed her tight around the waist, and covered her forehead and cheeks with warm kisses.

"What happened?" she asked. "I was just about to leave."

"I'm so sorry, babes," he breathed into her neck. "Customs. They detained me."

"What?" Jaylah searched his face. His eyes were bloodshot and tiny lines crisscrossed his forehead. His usually luminous dark skin appeared dull and ashen, and though he was always impeccably dressed, his clothes were disheveled. "Why would they detain you?"

"Being black with an African name can trigger these types of things. It's happened before, but they didn't give me a reason this time. They just kept me waiting, asked a lot of questions, and subjected me to several searches. I had to turn off my phone, which is why I couldn't let you know what was happening. I'm sorry for worrying you."

"It's okay," Jaylah said, kissing his cheek. "I'm glad you made it safely."

Johnny smiled the smile that usually caused Jaylah's clothes to fall off. "Well, I'm here and I've had a rough go of it, does this mean you'll tell me the news now?"

"Soon. I'm starving. Let's get out of here and get something to eat. I function a lot better on a full stomach."

"Sounds like a plan."

Jaylah slid her hand in his and led the way to the parking lot. Johnny had been a man of his word. She had asked him to travel 5,000 miles just to have a conversation and he'd shown up without hesitation. She wasn't sure what would happen to them, but in that moment, she felt like her father was right. Everything would turn out fine.

Jaylah and Johnny strolled along the cobblestone promenade of Fisherman's Village in Marina del Rey. After waiting all afternoon to eat, she gorged herself on jumbo shrimp, French fries, and the largest ice cream cone Johnny claimed to have ever seen.

Unlike Jaylah, he nibbled on his salmon trying not to leg jet lag and impatience overtake him. As they walked along the wharf, she knew he wanted to hear what she had to say, but took pleasure in making him wait just a little while longer.

"Thank you," she whispered when they stopped to stare at a boat trudging through the harbor.

Johnny wrapped his arms around her and she relaxed into his embrace. "For what?"

"For coming. For moving out. For putting up with my shit."

He kissed her cheek. "No worries, babes. I know you're testing me."

She stared up at him, surprised he'd caught on to her plan. "Testing you?"

"Yes. But I get it. I fucked up, and you're trying to see if I'll fuck up again."

He was right; Jaylah had been waiting to see if Johnny would falter. Would he lie to her again? Would he prove himself untrustworthy? Would he cheat on her the same way he'd stepped out on his wife?

"And will you?" she asked.

"No, I don't plan on it, babes."

You didn't plan on cheating on your wife with me, either. And you didn't plan on knocking me up, she wanted to tell him, but she gazed at the water instead.

Jaylah rested her head against Johnny's chest and imaged what their life would look like a year from now. She'd be a vet at *Glamour*, regularly crafting features for the website and the print magazine; they'd own stylish flat in Highbury that would house her books and his record collection; they'd go on dates to the theater or Ronnie Scott's; they'd make love every night because they couldn't keep their hands off each other; and somehow, despite their too-full life, she and Johnny would raise the most beautiful baby the world had ever seen.

"So, about what I said on the phone," Jaylah said, inching toward her news.

Jaylah could feel his body tense up beneath her; apparently Johnny was bracing for the worst as well.

"Yes?"

"I think..." she paused, stretching the moment out as long as possible. "I think I want to give it a shot."

He spun her around to face him. "You serious?" A smile shot across his handsome face before it turned serious again. "Wait, what does, 'give it a shot' mean'?"

"The baby. I'm going to have the baby, Johnny." She stared into his face, which grew into an enormous grin. "I just hope I'm making the right choice."

Jaylah started to cry. They were not just tears of joy; she was terrified, excited, and unsure of herself all at once. She'd thought about the blob, *her baby*, for the past few weeks, and although she wasn't sure she was ready to be a mother, Jaylah could never bring herself to make the appointment to end her child's life either.

Despite the pressure, she wasn't having this baby for her mother or Jourdan or even Johnny. She had made this choice on her own, based on her own gut instincts. No matter what happened between them, Jaylah knew she could pull this parenting thing off— even if she had to do it alone.

"Oh my God, Jaylah. Thank you. Thank you, thank you, thank you," Johnny found her mouth and thanked her with his tongue. When he pulled away, she noticed the corners of his eyes were damp.

"Are you crying?

"No," he laughed, wiping his face. "I was hoping you would keep the baby, but I wasn't sure you actually would. This is the happiest day of my life, Jaylah."

"Your entire life?" she asked, cocking an eyebrow.

"Yes, it's right up there with the day we rode the London Eye. That changed everything, innit."

He was right; that day had been the beginning of them. Before that afternoon she chalked up her attraction to him as fleeting and purely carnal, but after that day, she wanted to be an irreplaceable part of his world.

Had she willed this to happen? Jaylah would never have gotten pregnant on purpose, but the baby cemented her place in Johnny's life.

Today she was happy. Today she tried not to let her fears and doubts overtake her joy. Today she felt loved and cared for and protected. Had Johnny asked her to marry him again in that moment she would have said yes, but he hadn't.

And she was thankful.

Even though she'd agreed to have the baby, their relationship would still take work. Jaylah had to work to trust him again, work to take him at his word, and work to love him without conditions.

Before they left, Jaylah asked the Goddess of the Sea to give her the strength to put herself first—no matter what.

9

"Why don't you join me," Johnny said, patting the empty space on the bed.

Jaylah heard him in the distance, but was transfixed by the view of the ocean outside his window. A million thoughts fought for space inside her brain. How would she break the news of her pregnancy to her editor? Could she work until the day she gave birth? How much time would she need to take off? Would Johnny's divorce be final before their child was born? Would she even be a good mother?

Usually Jaylah was alone when she spiraled down the long and winding rabbit hole of her mind, but this time Johnny was there. And he wanted her attention.

Jaylah didn't mean to tune him out, but her brain would not shut off, no matter how much she wished it would.

He crossed the room, slung an arm around her waist, and kissed her on the neck. "What are you thinking about?"

"Everything," she said, wanting to keep her private thoughts to herself for a while. She knew Johnny loved her. She could tell by the way he looked at her, adoringly, like she was the sun breaking through a cloudy London day. But Jaylah also knew Johnny wanted her to just give in—to him, to his demands, their love affair—and she wasn't sure she could do that just yet.

Jaylah had dreams, big ones that sometimes scared the shit out of her, but also made her feel flat out alive. Moving to another country had always been a dream, but she suppressed it and instead put her head down and busted her ass at the *L.A. Weekly* hoping that one day she'd be able to spend a summer in Cape Town or jet to Paris to write about the influence of pop culture abroad.

That felt like eons ago. Three years after she'd graduated from NYU Jaylah had relegated her dreams to some hazy spot in the future that damn near disappeared from view. But then she got fired. And her life suddenly shifted in such a severe way she couldn't help but find the pieces of herself that had been scraped away by work, family, and her surrender to responsibility.

"Can't you do that later?" He skimmed the base of her neck with his lips and coaxed her back to reality. "It's been a while, innit?"

"Has it?"

"Yes. You've been upset with me, so a brotha's been cut off," he said, finding her lips, taking his time to linger over her full pout before kissing her. She could feel him trembling, perhaps even aching. It had been a weeks since they fused their bodies together and danced.

"Is that right?" she asked, already knowing the answer.

"Mmm hmm. But we can make up for lost time." Johnny caressed her breasts through the soft fabric of her dress, giving her nipple a playful pinch. "I don't plan on leaving this room for the next two days."

She turned to face him. "That's a lot of time indoors. How will you keep from getting bored?"

"Oh, I have a few ideas." He slipped her dress over her head and running his tongue along her collarbone.

"Leave it on," she commanded, grabbing for the gauzy fabric.

He stared at her confused. "Why?"

"I'm fat. Look at me." Jaylah threw her hands up, already self-conscious about her growing abdomen. "I'm only eight weeks along and I already look *so pregnant!*"

Johnny flung his head back and laughed. "We must be looking at two different people, innit." He took the dress and chucked it across the room. "You look stunning, as always, love."

"You're just saying that because you want some."

"Yes," he said, pressing into her, revealing the bulge straining against his zipper. "But also because it's the truth."

She eyed him in disbelief, refusing to completely yield to his touch, too busy caught up in her own head.

Before she could say anything else, Johnny scooped her up and carried Jaylah to the bed, placing her on the duvet as if she were a fragile box and he was scared to break whatever it contained. He straddled her legs, unclasping her bra and tossing it over his shoulder before leaning in to her nipples. They instinctively swelled as soon as his tongue grazed her skin, reminding her of how long it had actually been since they'd made love.

Too long, Jaylah's body seemed to moan in response to his touch, *way too damn long*.

Johnny slid her panties down and traced her legs in warm kisses until he got to the space between her thighs. He stuck his tongue into the damp opening, gently probing her walls and lapping up her nectar until Jaylah let out faint *ooohs* and *ahhhs*, cheering him on.

Jaylah stared down the length of her body and watched Johnny slurp her up until he found the spot, *that spot*, that made her writhe beneath him, begging for more. *Please, please, please* she thought, but could not get out more than a whimper. Instead, she moved her hips faster as the pressure grew in her loins, hoping Johnny would get the hint and climb inside her.

A growing rumble vibrated through Jaylah's body, threatening to take her over the edge. She bit her lip and enjoyed the sparks shooting through her belly. Johnny continued to drink her up until she let out a sharp breath, then released the pressure building in her body by screaming out his name like it was an ancient chant.

Johnny, Johnny, Johnny. Damn, Johnny.

Unable to wait any longer, he slid into her and moved in slow, deep circles, nibbling on her earlobe and whispering vulgar phases that excited her even more. She grabbed his ass, pulling him deeper into her body, fusing them together once again. Johnny's body felt like home, warm, familiar and welcoming of her touch.

"I love you, Jaylah," he panted between strokes that felt *so, so good* she could hardly concentrate. "I love you, girl. I love you."

He rolled Jaylah onto her side and entered her from behind, caressing her taut nipples and kissing her shoulder as he pounded into her. They moved together, keeping each other's rhythm as if nothing had gone wrong between them.

It had been weeks since they made love, weeks of arguing over phone lines and text messages, weeks of hurt feelings followed by promises that things would work out, weeks of doubts. But in that moment they were completely in sync, moving as a singular person being fueled by a singular craving.

Johnny slipped a finger inside her and rubbed Jaylah's clit as he moved within her. She felt an immediate sensation radiate through her body and the tension between her thighs multiplied tenfold, causing her to quake for a second time. He quickened his pace, and Jaylah braced herself for the orgasm quickly winding its way through her frame.

Then it happened. She lost control, convulsing as waves of passion crashed against her thighs, fingers, toes, breasts, and finally rushed to straight to her head. Johnny continued thrusting, tightly grabbing her hips and tugging a handful of Jaylah's hair until he let out a primal grunt and collapsed beside her.

They gasped for air, trying to recover from what had just transpired between them. His head lay across her back, and she turned to face him.

"I missed you, too," Jaylah said, touching the side of his smooth face.

Johnny chuckled. "But do you love me?"

"I wouldn't be here if I didn't."

"I don't know. You could be using me for my body," he teased.

"True, it *is* pretty awesome. I mean, did you see how you picked me up?" They laughed, and then slipped into the comfortable silence of satisfied, postcoital couples.

"So..." Jaylah hesitated, finally speaking up. "My parents want to meet you."

"Good. When?"

"Tomorrow. My mom is cooking 'a proper dinner,'" Jaylah said, mimicking her mother.

"Hmmm, sounds formal. I didn't bring a suit."

"You don't need a suit, they just want to know what kind of man you are."

"Did you tell them about..."

Jaylah looked at him like he was crazy. "Your wife?"

"My pending divorce," he corrected her.

"No. And we aren't going to, okay? That would be an invitation for them to hate you and you want to make a good impression."

"Then I better get a suit," he chortled. "I'm going to take a shower, then you can take me to find one, yeah?"

"I thought you weren't leaving this room for two days."

"Change of plans, babes." He kissed her. "But don't worry. That was only the beginning." Johnny winked then disappeared into the bathroom.

Only the beginning, she thought. *Of what?*

Jaylah hoped for good things, hoped her parents would love Johnny as much as she did, but she knew her mother would be tough to win over.

She prayed this was the beginning of their happy, drama-free life, but she knew they had a few more obstacles to clear before they could be one little blissful family. In her heart, she believed they could handle her parents, the baby, her job, and Johnny's divorce. But her mind, that thing that just wouldn't shut off, had its doubts.

Jaylah didn't know which one was right, but in that moment she knew she would follow her heart, wherever it lead.

10

"So, where do you want to go?" she asked once they were back in the car.

"Where can I get a good suit?"

"Depends. Do you want to drop a few hundred dollars at J.C. Penny, or a few thousand at Armani?"

Johnny scrunched up his face, "J.C. Penny? What's that?"

Jaylah chuckled, remembering how she used to love looking through Penny's overstuffed catalog as a child, picking out dresses and matching shiny shoes. She imagined Johnny thumbing through cheap suits, wondering if his tailor, yes, *his tailor*, could at least make the one he selected look like he'd gotten it from a mid-priced store.

"Never mind," she said, "I know you're more of a— how do you say?—smartly dressed bloke?"

Johnny nodded and Jaylah threw the car in gear, heading toward Rodeo Drive. He watched as she switched lanes, honking and mumbling curse words under her breath as traffic inched along Sepulveda Boulevard. She caught a glimpse of him shaking his head after she yelled at a driver who had cut her off.

"What?" she asked, changing lanes and glaring at yet another incompetent motorist.

He cracked an easy smile. "I've just never seen this side of you. You're almost as bad as the cabbies back home."

"Whatever," she said, sticking out her tongue. "I forgot how much I hate driving. I'm so used to taking the Tube now."

"Perhaps, you should get used to it again, yeah? As you get further along, I think I would feel more comfortable if you drove instead of took the train. Those things get stuck all the time. I would hate for you to be trapped underground and go into labor or something."

She cut her eyes at him. "You'd rather me go into labor while driving?"

"Of course not. I'd rather be there, but babies are unpredictable, innit?"

"I'm sure I'll be fine Johnny," she kissed her teeth. "You worry too much."

He reached across the seat and placed his hand on her stomach. "I have every right."

Fifteen minutes passed before either of them spoke again. Johnny gazed at Los Angeles whizzing by his window, while an annoying voice began gnawing at the corner of Jaylah's brain.

Don't take the Tube? What kind of crazy suggestion is that? the voice asked. *Be careful girl, it's only the beginning. He's trying to control you.*

Jaylah quieted the voice and reminded herself that men—good men like her father—doted on their women.

She'd seen it first hand. Though she was an only child, Jaylah's mother had been pregnant before. As a mater of fact, Jaylah had had a little brother—Julian-- when she was seven, but the baby died a month after he was born. The doctor said he'd passed away from SIDS.

"Just like that," he had said, snapping his fingers to demonstrate how her little brother's life could be snuffed out so suddenly.

Jaylah's mother was devastated. She took to her bed, grieving the loss of her son and barely tending to her daughter. For months, Jaylah watched as her father catered to her mother, cooking meals, cleaning the house, and rearranging his schedule at work to nurse Mrs. Baldwin back to herself. Jaylah's father also lavished his baby girl with attention, aware of how much of a toll her mother's depression was having on her little seven-year-old life.

Jaylah glanced over at Johnny. He certainly reminded her of her father. When her morning sickness had gotten so bad she was sprawled out on the couch for days, Johnny brought his office to her flat so he could still close deals while making sure she didn't become dehydrated again and end up in hospital. Despite their beginning, Johnny had been a man of his word. He showed up when he said he would, called daily to make sure she was okay, and if she ever needed to bury a body, she knew he'd be there with the shovel.

Johnny was a good man, but there was a thin line between concerned partner and controlling mate. She promised herself to pay attention to which side of the divide Johnny towed.

"Here we are," Jaylah said, breaking the quiet that had enveloped them. "You have just about every high end retailer here, want to try Neiman Marcus first?"

"I'm just the passenger, babes, you lead the way."

She parked the car behind the store, which took up an entire block, and she and Johnny made their way inside.

As soon as they entered Neiman Marcus Jayleh felt underdressed, the £20 floral maxi dress and jean jacket she picked up at Cafe Vintage seemed too boho for such an elegant space. She watched the sales associates, dressed in crisp black suits and sensible heels, size her up then dismiss her as too poor to shop in their venerable store. They were partially right. Jaylah's budget was more suited for bargain hunting and sample sales than spending thousands of dollars on a Givenchy bag. But there was no harm in browsing, right?

The first floor of the department store glistened with its polished marble floors, ambient lighting, and stately glass cases full of wares Jaylah could scarcely afford. As usual, Johnny strode through the store confident he belonged. Unlike Jaylah, he often bought things without looking at the price, never glanced at the check before whipping out his credit card to pay a bill, and regularly spent more on a perfectly tailored suit than she paid in rent.

Jaylah enjoyed the fruits of Johnny's labor, never having to pay for a beer, a dinner, or a night out when they were together, but their unequal financial footing made her nervous.

Now that they were expecting a child would he insist she give up her career under the guise of being concerned for the baby? Would he use his money to control her life, her decisions? Would she become so dependent upon him that she couldn't afford to leave, even if it were necessary?

Jaylah vowed she'd keep her *In Case Shit Happens* account fully funded, just in case she needed to make an escape; she refused to be trapped.

They had been in the store for ten minutes and not one clerk had given them more than a passing glance.

They were no closer to finding the men's department, so Johnny took the lead. They walked toward a woman rearranging gold watches in a display case and waited for her to acknowledge them. When she didn't even look up, Johnny spoke up.

"Pardon me, ma'am," he said, deploying the formal British accent he usually reserved for business. Jaylah watched as the woman's expression changed from annoyed to enamored once she finally looked at Johnny. As she padded toward them, the gaunt woman curled a wisp of blonde hair behind her ear and smiled a little too wide for Jaylah's liking.

"How can I help you, sir?" she said, ignoring Jaylah.

"I'm looking for the men's department. Where might I find it?"

"Take the escalators all the way up to the top floor," she said, sticking out her chest and showing all of her chemically whitened teeth.

"Brilliant. Thank you."

Ugh, even the sales clerks are soooo L.A., Jaylah thought.

"Would you like me to show you, sir?" the blonde asked, running a hand across her cleavage, as they turned to leave.

"No, no. I'm sure we can sort it out from here. Thank you again," Johnny said, smiling at the blonde.

Jaylah held her tongue until they got on the escalator. She was used to women fawning over Johnny while they were out, he was gorgeous after all, and in London, black men like him (well-mannered, moneyed, gorgeous) rarely had unambiguously black women on their arms. The difference? Usually the women back home had the decency to at least acknowledge her while they shamelessly flirted with her man.

"Would you like me to show you?" Jaylah mocked the clerk's valley girl tone. "I'm sure she wasn't talking about the men's department. Did you see the way she was looking at you? Ugh."

"Really? I didn't notice."

"Yeah, sure you didn't. That type of thing happens like every time we go out. How can you not notice it?"

"I don't know, I'm used to it I guess," he shrugged like someone had asked him about the weather and he'd said, *I don't know, mate, looks like rain.*

"Humble, much?"

Johnny chuckled and placed his hand on the small of Jaylah's back as they transferred from one escalator to another. "That's not what I meant. Women have always been nice to me."

"Johnny there's nice, and then there's attempted seduction. She was flirting with you like I wasn't even there. Who did she think I was? Your sister?" Jaylah said, irritated he didn't seem to be troubled by the scene.

"It's all the same to me, I suppose. I'm not the one doing the flirting so it doesn't bother me."

"Of course it doesn't bother *you*, you're not the one watching your partner get hit on by pretty women."

"She was pretty?" Johnny teased, craning his neck toward the bottom of the escalator. "And I am the one at times. I've seen how men look at you, babes, especially when you're wearing a tight dress. Mmm!" He brought his fingers to his lips, then kissed them like an Italian chef tasting something good. "But as long as they don't cross the line, it doesn't bother me."

"Well, you won't have to worry about all that. Soon, I'll be huge."

"I know," he said, putting his hand to her stomach and grinning. "I can't wait."

Jaylah watched Johnny move through the men's department as if he was a seasoned fashion expert, and in many ways he was. He knew what worked on his toned body, and quickly brushed off suggestions that would not compliment his six-foot-two-inch frame.

"I prefer a British cut suit," she heard him tell the salesman. "You know, two buttons, nipped in at the waist?"

The pair sorted through endless rows of dark colored ensembles, looking for one that was suitable enough for meeting her parents. Jaylah took a seat and eyed Johnny as he picked through the racks, handing off several options to the clerk before checking out the shirts.

Jaylah loved watching him, that's how she'd spotted him the first night, dancing under the flickering lights of the Mau Mau Bar. From the moment she saw him across the room keeping time with the beat, she couldn't take her eyes off of him.

Gorgeous. Intense. Cocksure. She was drawn to Johnny's quiet confidence and his ability to dominate the space, any space, without even trying.

Nothing had changed since that first night.

Back in her flat she'd sit in bed and watch him get dressed for work. After spending the night, he'd emerge from the shower with a towel tightly wrapped around his abdomen and begin shaving his face with the precision of a seasoned barber.

"What?" He'd asked her once when he noticed Jaylah staring at him. "Did I miss a spot?"

She'd laughed at the thought of it. "Nah."

"Then why are you looking at me like that?"

"Like what?" she said, cocking her head to the side to take him in at a new angle.

"Like you're sizing me up." He crossed the room to sweep his lips across hers before tasting her tongue.

Jaylah shrugged and smiled. "Just because..." she told him, holding back the urge to say she hoped this was how they would be forever.

Johnny sauntered over to her, dress shirts in hand, and placed a sloppy kiss on her forehead. "Be right back, yeah? I'm going to try these on."

She nodded and watched him disappear into the dressing room.

Johnny is buying a suit to meet my parents. That means something right?

Sure he said he loved her, jumped on a plane and flew 5,000 miles because she insisted they speak in person, and was careful to update her about the changes in his life, but what did that really mean? And more importantly, what did she want it to mean?

The fact remained—Johnny was still *married.*

The word rolled through her brain like a freight train threatening to derail her dreams of happily ever after.

Yes, he'd moved out of his house and had taken her with him to see the solicitor, but that didn't *mean* anything right now. Johnny and Fiona had been married for four years and were together throughout most of their time at University. Every memory he had from college, every family gathering he'd attended for the last decade, and every time he'd made love before they met, Fiona had been by his side.

How could she compete with that?

Their affair had been a powerful whirlwind, consuming them both at breakneck speed and uprooting the course of their lives. But Johnny was still married, and people changed their minds about getting divorced all the time. How could she be sure he wouldn't do the same?

No matter how wonderful he treated her now, Jaylah was uncertain if they could recover from their beginning, from his lie. He had purposely let her fall for him, wooing her with his impeccable charm and the promise of coupledom, knowing full well he had already promised Fiona forever.

Just a few months ago she floated through London feeling like she'd struck the lotto. After years of hating her life she finally had it all—dream job, new best friend, and a man who adored her. That afternoon in Brick Lane had felt like confirmation that everything she'd gone through—every shitty assignment, run-in with her mother, every asshole she'd dated—had prepared her for that moment. All of her troubles had made getting what she wanted feel that much sweeter.

Jaylah's life was going so ridiculously well that she could hardly believe it when she overheard a man ask Johnny about his wife. And instead of correcting him, Johnny had calmly told the man about Fiona's trip to Scotland and promised they'd all get together once she returned.

His wife? Johnny was married? she thought as she listened to their conversation that day.

Her brain couldn't comprehend it, and the entire idea seemed down right asinine, until she watched his face collapse in on itself when she confronted him. Then she knew.

Johnny was not only married, but he was a liar. And how could they recover from that?

The question made her nauseous. Jaylah glanced around for a restroom, already feeling the bile inch its way up her throat. She asked the clerk to point her to the ladies' room, and raced downstairs to release the contents of her stomach.

Jaylah barely made it to the stall. She felt like someone had taken out her stomach and shaken everything free. She heaved up chunks of shrimp, and salad, and ice cream from her afternoon meal and her body continued to retch until Jaylah felt like she had been completely wrung out.

She waited for a few moments to catch her breath, and to make sure nothing else would come spewing forth, before heading to the sink to wash her hands and splash water on her face. While she scooped up handfuls of the cool liquid to rinse out her mouth, Jaylah heard a voice.

"Are you okay, sweetheart?" an elderly woman asked, lines of concern creasing her face.

Jaylah nodded, then shrugged her shoulders, offering an apology. "Yeah, sorry. Morning sickness."

The woman's face softened into a smile. "Oh! How far along?"

"About nine weeks. Feels like nine years already," Jaylah said, trying to mirror the woman's smile, but she was too spent.

"Hang in there, sweetie. You're almost past the worst part," the woman said before patting Jaylah on the back and walking out the door.

Although she knew the woman was talking about her morning sickness, Jaylah hoped she was right. She hoped the worst part of her relationship with Johnny, his lie and her unwillingness to completely trust him, was over and they could move on with their lives.

But she wasn't convinced; and it was killing her.

11

When she was eight, Jaylah's mother spotted her stuffing a handful of salt water taffy chews in her pocket during a trip to the grocery store. As they moved through the aisles, Mrs. Baldwin eyed her daughter to see if her conscience would kick in before they left, but when it was apparent Jaylah planned on walking out without paying for the candy her mother stepped in.

"Jay Jay," Mrs. Baldwin said, "What's in your pocket?"

"Nothing, mama," Jaylah said instinctively, unaware her mother saw her swipe the treats.

Mrs. Baldwin put her hands on her hips, then crouched down to meet her daughter's eyes. "Are you sure? Because it looks like there's something in that one," she said pointing to Jaylah's right pocket.

Jaylah's eyes grew wide, but she stuck to her story. "It's just..." She stared at her mother's stoic face, "It's just some lint, mama."

"Hmph," Mrs. Baldwin said, crossing her arms. "It looks like something's in your pocket, sweetie. But since you say it's not," Mrs. Baldwin hunched her shoulders and stood up, "okay."

Jaylah remembered feeling like she was going to explode, the air in her lungs exacting pressure on her little chest because breathing might give her away. Then it happened, her mother said something that rocked her eight-year-old self to the core.

"I'm so glad you know better than to lie to me," she said, putting her groceries on the checkout belt like everything was normal. "Lies are always worse than the truth, Jay Jay. And liars?" Jaylah's mom kissed her teeth and shook her head in disgust, "liars are the worst kind of people; you can't trust them. And if you can't trust them," she turned to look at her daughter, "how can you love them?"

The thought of losing her mother's love sent a chill from her pigtails to her L.A. Gear sneakers. Suddenly her school cardigan felt like it was made of itchy wool, and her plaid romper felt two sizes too small.

Although Jaylah was a tomboy who preferred jeans over dresses, she still wanted to be just like her mother. Graceful, petite, and strikingly beautiful. Somehow

TWO STEPS BACK

all of Sarah's genes had skipped right over her daughter and scattered into her cousins who looked more like they belonged to Mrs. Baldwin than Jaylah did. For starters, Mrs. Baldwin was a red bone, at least that's what Jaylah's dad had called her on one of their vacations to Florida. It happened because Mrs. Baldwin insisted on lying by the pool, "To get some color back in my cheeks," she'd said, but her husband had his doubts.

"C'mon Sarah, you know you a red bone. That's about all the color you're gonna get. You better get under an umbrella before you mess around and get burnt!" he said, chuckling to himself.

Hearing her father's advice, Jaylah had stayed under an umbrella or a cabana or on in the shadow of a balcony all weekend until her father asked why she wasn't doing belly flops in the pool.

"I don't wanna get burnt," she said, looking into the mirror that was her father's face, "like mama."

Jaylah's father brushed off her worries. "Your mama's a red bone baby girl..."

"So am I daddy," she interrupted, "I'm just like mama."

"Nawl, sweetie, you're like me, you know, the color of the earth. We can stay out in the sun as much as we want. Now go on, enjoy yourself, baby girl."

The idea that Jaylah was not like her mother did not make sense to her little girl brain.

How could she *not* be like her mother? The thought made her panic and seek out Mrs. Baldwin's approval at every turn. So the incident in the grocery store had seemed significantly riskier after her mother's soul-stirring tidbit about trust and love.

Jaylah did not want her mother to think she was a liar because they were already so unlike one another—different faces, different eyes, different skin—

she couldn't bear losing her mother's love as well.

When Mrs. Baldwin finished loading all of her groceries on the belt, Jaylah reached in her pocket and pulled out the candies.

"Sorry mama." She held them out to her mother, her eyes on the verge of tears.

Mrs. Baldwin plucked two candies from Jaylah's hand and told the cashier to ring them up, before sliding them in her purse. When they were done loading the groceries into the car, Mrs. Baldwin took out the taffy chews and gave one to Jaylah.

"Remember what I said, Jay Jay. Liars are the worse kind of people because you can't trust them. And if you can't trust them..." she paused.

"You can't love them," Jaylah said on cue.

"Exactly, Jay Jay. Exactly."

Mrs. Baldwin's words flashed through Jaylah's mind as she made her way back to the men's department to find Johnny.

Liars are the worst kind of people. You can't love them.

Johnny had lied to her about his wife, but there was no doubt in her mind that she loved him.

But was she supposed to?

The thought fluttered through her brain, but when she saw him standing in front of a three-way mirror wearing a navy blue suit that hugged his body so well she was almost jealous, she forced it out of her mind.

"You look good," she said, bushing an imaginary a piece of lint from his shoulder. "*Really* good."

He turned to face her, already smiling, but his expression changed when he looked into her eyes. "What's the matter?"

"Nothing. Just a little tired," she said, sweeping aside his concern. But the truth was that scene in the bathroom had tuckered her out and all Jaylah wanted to do at that very moment was lie down, watch TV, and eat copious amounts of chocolate.

"But your eyes are red and you look a little…"

Jaylah waved him off as if he were imagining things. "I'm fine. I just need to grab a quick snack."

"Already? My boy is going to be strong!"

She rolled her eyes. "Whatever. My stomach is a bit unsettled, that's all."

He looked in her eyes again and seemed to examine her face for clues. "Still? Did you…"

"A little, but I'm fine, I just need…"

"What's a little? Did anything stay down?"

She didn't answer. Jaylah knew if she told him that *everything* she'd eaten had come roaring back up her esophagus he would overreact. And that wouldn't help either of them.

"Forget the suit," Johnny said, removing the jacket and leading her to a nearby seat. "Let's go back to the hotel so you can get some rest."

"I'm fine, babe. I'll sit here while you try on the rest of them. I'll be okay. Promise."

He hesitated, seeming to run her words through his head before he spoke. "No need. I think I'm done anyway. This is my favorite of the lot."

"You sure? You're not just saying that because you're trying to rush are you?"

He cracked a wide grin. "Look at me, babes." Johnny spun around like a spokesmodel, "I look like a boss, innit?"

Jaylah grinned in spite of herself. Johnny *did* look damn good. The jacket showed off his broad shoulders and tapered waist, and the pants skimmed his legs but didn't hug them. He looked like a sable-skinned James Bond and would certainly show her bourgie mother that he had his shit together and could afford to take care of her daughter.

Johnny leaned down and tilted Jaylah's chin up so he could meet her lips. "Be right back."

He disappeared into the dressing room once again, but Jaylah only briefly reclined and closed her eyes for a few short minutes before he returned.

"That was fast," she said when she saw him walking toward her. Johnny held out his hand and she took it, then walked with him to pay for the suit.

The sales clerk was all smiles now, no doubt bolstered by the prospect of a fat commission. In addition to the suit, Johnny had picked out a crisp white shirt and striking red tie. The total made Jaylah woozy. $2476.43.

Jaylah could probably live on that amount for over a month and a half, easily paying her rent, keeping herself fed, and even buying a pair of earrings or a blouse at one of the Portobello Road Markets. But for Johnny it was nothing at all, just another garment he would wear to close the deal and secure Jaylah for himself.

They strolled hand-in-hand out of the men's department, through the store, and to a café near the store. Johnny insisted Jaylah eat before attempting the drive back to the hotel, so she took him to one of her favorite Italian delis in Beverly Hills.

Every time Jaylah had been to Ferrarini she could never decide what to order. The glass vitrines were filled with colorful deserts, buttery pastries, and some of the freshest meats in the city. There were so many choices it would sometimes take Jaylah fifteen full minutes to decide what she wanted.

Johnny waited as she scanned the menu, tempted to order one of everything and take it back to the hotel.

"Can I help you, miss?" The dark-haired barista smiled at her from across the counter, and Jaylah considered flirting with the stranger.

"Coffee. I want coffee," she said, enticed by the robust aromas percolating just behind the handsome man.

"What kind of coffee, miss? We have Americanos, cappuccinos, espressos, an Ethiopian blend that's really good..."

Jaylah was about to place her order, but Johnny interrupted. "No coffee. She can't have any right now." Jaylah made a face, like, *what are talking about, fool?* But he was unmoved. "The baby, remember? I read caffeine isn't good for the baby."

"You read what?" she said, irritated he was vetoing her chance at a cup of Joe. First her mother had admonished her for wanting some, running down a list of things she could no longer enjoy if she wanted to birth a healthy baby, now Johnny was picking up where Mrs. Baldwin left off and was being a food Nazi too?

Jaylah groaned her displeasure. "Johnny, one cup won't hurt. It's no like I'm going to drink a whole pot of the stuff."

He shook his head. "I don't think it's a good idea, especially with the morning sickness. You already vomited up everything you ate, you really want to press your luck?"

"Not *everything.*" Jaylah stared at Johnny and he cocked an eyebrow, indicating he wasn't falling for her bullshit. "Fine," she gave in.

Jaylah turned her attention to the barista who pretended not to witness the couple's brief spat. "Can I have a peppermint tea and a prosciutto and mozzarella sandwich?"

"Sure! And you, sir?"

"Two chocolate croissants and a bottle of water."

It was Jaylah's turn to raise her 'brow. "*Two?*"

Johnny let a smirk dance across his lips. "I know you."

Even though she was peeved he'd put the kibosh on her chance at a cup of coffee, the truth was, he *did* know her—well. Chocolate was one of her biggest weaknesses, and she knew he was using the promise of a pastry as an apology of sorts. She couldn't have coffee, but as long as he didn't try to cut off her chocolate, she just might make it through this pregnancy.

They grabbed a seat facing Burton Way and waited for their food to arrive.

"You know, pregnant women have coffee all the time, right? It's not even considered bad anymore."

"I'm not concerned about *pregnant women,*" he said, stroking the back of her hand with his fingers. "I'm concerned about you. I just want you to be okay. I already lost one baby, Jaylah, and I don't want to go through that again."

Oh shit, Jaylah remembered. *Fiona had lost their child.*

Her pregnancy was the reason they'd finally decided to wed after years of being together. "I had to do the right thing," he'd told her one night while they lay in bed. "What kind of man would I be if I didn't?"

Jaylah wondered if the baby had survived if she'd been sitting with Johnny now. Would he have even let them happen? Or would he have neglected to call after the night they met and made out in his car?

A sickening thought crawled down her spine and caused her to shudder. *What would happen if I lost this baby?*

She hated to ask, hated to even think about their relationship coming to an end, or the amorphous blob she'd suddenly grown attached to not making it into the world, but she had to know. She couldn't leave anything up to chance.

"What if something *did* happen to the baby, Johnny?" she asked, staring out the window trying not to look at him. "Would you leave me too?

The question landed like a bomb, exploding hurt feelings and rendering them both silent. She peeked at him from the corner of her eye and saw a wave of shock—or was it hurt?—move across his handsome face.

"I...I...don't even want to..." he stuttered, then stopped; the question robbing him of his voice yet again. "Why are you thinking like this?"

"You married Fiona because she got pregnant." She looked at him then. "But she lost the baby. Now you're getting divorced. What if..."

He held up his hand. "A lot happened between those two events, Jaylah. We're not getting divorced because she lost the baby. That was almost five years ago. We just grew—"

"Right," she cut him off hoping to sidestep the standard line of a relationship pulled apart by time and unhappiness. "You're getting divorced because of me. I'm the home wrecker, remember?"

She meant that last bit as a half-joke, but plump tears ran to the rims of her eyes after she said it.

Home wrecker.

That's what Jaylah was, right? She'd never actually said the words aloud, but she'd thought them—almost nonstop—since that afternoon in Brick Lane. How else could she describe falling in love with a married man, who in turn had decided to leave his wife because she was carrying his child?

If Jaylah hadn't stepped in and wrecked Fiona's life, wouldn't she be at home with her husband?

"Jaylah," Johnny said, his tone soft and careful. "You're not a home wrecker, love. I admit, I was completely taken with you and lost my head, but this isn't your fault."

"But if you hadn't have met me, you wouldn't be getting divorced and Fiona wouldn't be losing her husband."

Johnny took a sip of water and appeared to compose his thoughts. It was his turn to glance at the traffic humming along outside of the café. "We would have gotten divorced anyway, Jay."

"Yeah, just not so soon," she said dryly.

"Does it matter when? Our relationship was over, had been over for years. We were just both too comfortable and too scared to say the words. Meeting you was the catalyst for me to finally do what I'd thought about doing so many times before."

"But you were still sleeping with her..." Jaylah half-asked/half-stated before really thinking about the implication of her words. But it was one of the things that continued to gnaw at her brain.

Had she ever actually shared Johnny? Did he sleep with both of them at the same time? Had there been some tiny sliver of overlap between the times he shared her bed and when he made love to his wife?

Made love...to Fiona?

The mere thought of it triggered the bile to percolate in Jaylah's belly.

It shouldn't have mattered considering they hadn't even talked about being exclusive when they first started dating. But there had been no one else in Jaylah's orbit after Johnny swept into her world and set her heart alight. She didn't even notice other men when she moved through the city; he had captured her attention so thoroughly she was blind to everyone else.

But could the same be said for him, especially with a wife at home?

Johnny rubbed the side of his head and sighed. "No. Not since…"

"We met? I found out I was pregnant? What?" Jaylah pressed, scared of what he might say.

He flinched at her sharp tone, and his chest billowed like someone had flipped a switch. "Since that afternoon on the London Eye," he said grabbing her hand and exhaling when Jaylah didn't pull it away. "That was the beginning…of us."

Jaylah inspected his face for anything that would tell her Johnny was bullshitting her. A twitch of the eye, the hint of a nervous smile, a diverted glace, but he never broke her gaze. Johnny stared into her eyes until she was forced to look away as a new groundswell of tears marched to her eyes once again.

Between the pregnancy hormones, and her unwillingness to give in and trust him, this situation was kicking her ass and forcing her to ride the wildest emotional rollercoaster of her life.

On one hand Jaylah was happy to have a man who loved her so fucking hard he'd jump on a plane and fly across an ocean because she said so, but on the other, nothing about their life—except for the inexplicable bond they'd created—made sense or felt like the responsible thing to do.

Jaylah had literally sprinted away from Johnny when she found out he was married. She had run for blocks and blocks trying to put enough space between the tug of her heart and what she knew was right, but it had all failed.

Despite her ranting, despite cursing him out for lying, despite refusing to take his calls, she was not only carrying his child, but she was also hoping against hope that they could survive this topsy-turvy ride. Jaylah took large gulps of her tea, wishing to quell the hurricane of feelings swirling around inside her head. Being constantly on edge was not good for her, but it was especially bad for the baby who was probably dinning on a womb full of cortisol.

If she was going to make through this Jaylah needed to get her shit together—fast. She couldn't vacillate between being head-over-tits in love with Johnny, to questioning every word that came out of his mouth. Even if she couldn't get her heart in check for her own peace of mind, she owed it to the little one growing inside her.

Jaylah started to speak, but the barista appeared with her sandwich and Johnny's croissants, causing her mouth to water as soon as she caught a whiff of the decadent pastries.

"Want a bite?" Johnny asked, a hopeful smile crossing his face. He held out the treat and fed it to Jaylah, his grin growing wider as he watched her do a little happy dance in her seat.

"Ohmygod," Jaylah said, eyes still closed. "That's soooo good, Johnny. So, so good. Give me more!"

Johnny shook his head playfully. "Not until you eat your sandwich, babes. Real food first, then sweets."

Damn, here he goes again.

Jaylah scrunched up her face and frowned at him. "You know, you may be older than me, but you're not my father. You can't tell me what to do. First the coffee, what's next? You're gonna tell me to eat all my vegetables before I can leave the table?"

He broke out in a hearty laugh, rocking back and forth as he chortled. His chuckle traveled across the table, softening Jaylah's expression into a smirk.

"*Believe me,*" he said, drawing out the words, "I know I can't tell you what to do, babes."

"Then what's up with the whole Jonathan Poku, Captain of the Food Police, thing?"

"I just want to take care of you, Jaylah," he said without a hint of a leftover laugh in his voice. "Is that alright with you?"

She stared at him for a beat, trying to decide if he was sincere. Giving into his words, Jaylah moved to his side of the table and sat in his lap. "Of course," she said, planting a soft kiss on his lips. "Of course that's alright."

12

Mrs. Baldwin scurried around the kitchen grabbing pans, flour, eggs, meat, and what looked like all of the produce from the fridge. Jaylah watched her mother, animated and frazzled, flutter about the space like a chicken running from a butcher's blade.

"Mom, it's not even noon. You don't have to start cooking yet," Jaylah said even though she knew her mother wasn't going to listen.

She'd seen this scene play out many times before whenever her father would bring over business associates, or Mrs. Baldwin would host luncheons for the women from their church. Jaylah's mom would easily spend an entire day cooking and cleaning in the hopes that everything would turn out perfect.

Watching her now, Jaylah felt both sorry for and in awe of her mother who worked so hard to keep up the façade of perfection that it had become her fulltime job. In Jaylah's 28 years, she had only seen her mother spin out of control once—when Julian died.

But even that didn't last very long. After Mrs. Baldwin recovered from losing her newborn, she poured herself into making sure everything in her life hummed along like a well-oiled machine.

For starters Sarah Baldwin always looked flawless. Even though she was over fifty, people often mistook her for Jaylah's older sister. Her skin unmarked by wrinkles, her petite frame still lean and toned, and her curly afro dyed blonde to cover up the gray. Mrs. Baldwin never left the house in sweats or "old lady clothes," as she called them. Instead she ran errands in tailored jeans, colorful blouses, and ballet flats.

"You should always look like you care, Jay Jay," she'd told her daughter once when she caught Jaylah on her way to the store wearing pajama bottoms and a hoodie, "even when you don't."

Despite hosting this dinner to interrogate Johnny, Jaylah marveled at her mother's need to impress him as well. She'd spent the morning plying Jaylah with questions about what Johnny ate, what he did for a living, and if his parents were excited about the baby.

"We haven't told them yet, mother," Jaylah had said, unable to tell her mother the truth. Not only did

Johnny's parents not know about the baby, they didn't even know about her.

"Do you need any help, mom?" she asked, hoping Mrs. Baldwin would turn her down. Though Jaylah didn't mind helping out, the last thing she wanted to do was hang out in the kitchen inhaling conflicting aromas while Mrs. Baldwin prepped the meal. Her stomach had been so finicky lately, any wayward smell could ruin her day and send her clinging to the porcelain throne.

"No, Jay Jay, I've got it covered. Besides, you're looking a little flush. Feeling okay?"

"Yeah...for now. I'm hoping I don't get sick, though. Yesterday I barely kept any food down."

Mrs. Baldwin emptied her arms and put the back of her hand to Jaylah's forehead. "Hmmm. Maybe you should make an appointment with Dr. Lawson just to make sure everything's alright. And I'm sure your..." she hesitated for a moment. "I'm sure Johnny would like to see the baby move if he can."

"Maybe. I'm going to get some air. You sure you don't need my help?"

"I can handle it. Just remember, dinner's at six."

"Got it."

Jaylah grabbed a bottle of water from the refrigerator then headed out the kitchen, excited to see her man. If she hurried, she could spend a few hours wrapped around Johnny instead of feeling guilty for not helping her mother with dinner.

Jaylah looked herself over in the living room mirror before leaving the house. She looked presentable *enough* in her baby doll dress and patterned tights, not that Johnny ever cared what she had on as long as he could peal it off.

Her hair was a different story, however. Her curls looked dry and frizzy, and in desperate need of a trim. Instead of climbing the stairs to her room, Jaylah smoothed her tresses into a lazy topknot, then bounded out the door and jumped in the car starting toward Marina del Rey. Fifteen minutes later she was knocking on Johnny's door.

"You're a little early for dinner, yeah?" Johnny asked, chuckling when he saw her standing in the entryway.

"Oh, you're not happy to see me?" she shot back, copping a fake attitude.

"Always, babes."

Johnny leaned down to kiss her, but Jaylah sidestepped his lips, walked around him, and stripped off her clothes.

"Not wasting any time today, huh?" he said, watching her remove her leggings.

"Oh please, Johnny," she said, taking her dress off. "It's not even like that. I just came to lie down. This bed is so damn comfortable."

Jaylah slid under the fluffy duvet and sighed. The supple sheets and feathery pillows were a welcomed change from the mattress at her parent's house that felt like she was sleeping on a concrete slab.

"Feeling okay?" he asked, slipping in beside her.

"Yeah, just tired. And a little concerned about tonight."

The truth? Jaylah was scared shitless about the dinner with her parents. She'd spent the previous night running the many ways their meal could turn into a disaster through her mind. The options were plentiful.

"Don't worry," he said, planting a kiss on her forehead, "your parents will love me. How could they not?"

She gave him a look.

Seriously?!

"Umm, I don't know, maybe because you're married? I'm almost certain that topic will come up."

"But I thought you haven't told them," Johnny asked, confused.

"Oh, I haven't. And I'm not going to," she added quickly. "But I'm sure my parents are going to ask about your 'plans,' and that's just code for, 'When are you guys getting married?'"

Jaylah could almost sense when the question would arise: most likely after dinner while her mother was serving the dessert. Her father would lean back in his chair, pat his too full stomach and ask, "So what are you two planning to do?" and Jaylah's mother would chime in, "Because the baby will be here before you know it."

She had been rehearsing her response for days.
Jaylah would speak up first, giving herself some wiggle
room to decide about their future after the baby arrived. Her parents wouldn't like her answer, but she'd
sell it on the basis of not wanting to rush into marriage
until well after her crazy pregnancy hormones wore off.
"Marriage shouldn't be a rash decision," she pictured
herself telling them. "I don't want to enter into it
lightly and while I'm not thinking straight," she'd reit-
erate.

Jaylah hoped they'd buy it.

"Well...you know my answer to that," Johnny said,
bringing her back to reality.

"Right, right. Get married, raise the baby, live happily ever after, the end," she said, her voice sounding
robotic.

"You make it sound like the worst thing in the
world."

"Well...it's not the best."

Lines of concern instantly crinkled Johnny's face.
"Excuse me? Not the best? You don't want to be with
me?"

"Of course I do," Jaylah said, hoping to lessen the
blow she just delivered. "I just don't want to rush into
anything, you know that. Besides, you're still married,
and unless the UK has some relaxed polygamy laws,
we can't get married right now even if we wanted to."

"But do you want to?" he asked, perched on an elbow and looking serious. "Because you know what I want."

Jaylah had to stop herself from rolling her eyes, but she was already annoyed. She'd come to Johnny's room to rest, not exert her mental reserves having the same damn conversation about their future for the fifty-leventh time.

How can you be so fucking sure? The words circled through her brain, but never made it to Jaylah's tongue. She didn't feel like having this discussion because neither of their views had changed over the past few weeks. Johnny's position was steadfast and unchanging, while everything about Jaylah was completely up in the air.

It was true, Jaylah couldn't picture her life without Johnny in it, and she'd certainly tried. But that didn't mean they should rush into marriage as soon as possible, did it? They hadn't even known each other for a year.

"Johnny..." she said, trying to choose her words carefully, "I don't know what I want right now. All I know is that I love you and we're having a baby. But other than that? I'm not even sure. I mean, your family doesn't know about me or the baby or your divorce. How can you even talk about marrying me and they don't even know I exist?"

"I've just been looking for the perfect time to tell them about everything. My family is very traditional, and..."

And they'll see me as some kind of home wrecking, American whore, she wanted to add, but didn't.

Jaylah rolled away from Johnny, turning her back on the rest of his explanation, which made her feel like a dirty secret he was scared to admit.

"Jaylah, don't be like that. Look at me, please?" he asked, trying to nudge her back in his direction, but she waved him off.

"I'm tired," she said, hoping he'd leave her alone. "I just want to take a nap."

Jaylah closed her eyes and tried to pretend Johnny wasn't lying next to her full of excuses about why he hadn't told his parents about the woman he professed to love and for whom he would uproot his entire life.

What part of the game is that? I'm good enough to impregnate, but not meet your traditional-ass parents?

What was he waiting for? The time would never be right. Waiting another day or month or year would not make telling the truth any easier, but it was clear to Jaylah that Johnny wasn't prepared to say it.

She felt herself losing the battle against the hurt building in her chest and squeezed her eyes tighter. But it was no use, Jaylah was crying, again. Silent tears streamed down her face and into the pillow faster than she could wipe them away, but she remained still, hoping Johnny wouldn't notice.

"Jaylah please look at me," he asked again, still trying to convince her to turn around. "I'm going to tell them, I prom—"

A sob escaped; she just couldn't hold it in any longer. Jaylah didn't want to hear any bullshit promises; she didn't want to hear that Johnny would tell his parents *soon, baby soon.* If she was going to do this and be with him for real and forever, he needed to claim her to those that mattered most.

"Baby?" Johnny moved to her side of the bed and saw Jaylah's damp face. "Please don't cry, Jay. You know I can't handle that." He cupped her face in his hands and kissed her tears.

She pulled away from him again, sitting up in bed and pulling her knees close to her chest. She didn't want Johnny to touch her, didn't want to lose sight of her hurt and anger by giving into his comforting hands.

Jaylah was pissed off, but lately, everything she felt manifested as tears, making her look like some kind of feeble, downtrodden woman who needed to be saved, which couldn't be further from the truth.

"Honestly, Johnny, I don't want to hear another fucking word about getting married until you tell your parents about us." She glared at him, wiping the remaining tears from her cheeks. "Not tonight, not tomorrow, not another fucking word!"

Her tone made him recoil. Johnny no doubt expected to soothe her with more promises, more declarations of love, but Jaylah wasn't having it. Not any-more. She was tired of feeling like a secret addiction that he'd accommodate, but not admit in the light of day.

Sure, they'd roamed around London like a happy couple, but she wasn't integrated into his life. Johnny had never introduced her to his friends, had never in-vited her up to his office, and had yet to tell his family he was in love with her.

Johnny stared at Jaylah, stunned, and she took ad-vantage of his silence.

"I've never met a single person you know, Johnny. Do you realize that? Not a *single* person. I know your parents moved back to Ghana, but you've got a sister in Manchester. That's like two hours away! Haven't met her. Haven't been introduced to anyone you work with. Haven't met any of your friends," she got out of bed and began pacing around the room. "Meanwhile, You've hung out with me and Jourdan, you've met my boss, and now you're meeting my parents. Do you know why that is?" she paused and waited for a re-sponse, but Johnny was rendered mute. "Because I fucking *care* about you. I love you. You're an im-portant part of my life, Johnny, so I've included you in it. I'm not stashing you away like something I'm ashamed of."

He came alive then. "I'm not ashamed of you, Jaylah."

"Oh really?" She threw back her head and laughed. "And how would I know that exactly?" she asked, crossing her arms and glowering at him.

"Because I love you, and—"

She cut him off, shaking her head. "Words. Those are just words, Johnny."

"Just words? So you don't think I love you?"

"You know what I learned back in my writing classes in college?"

"What does that have to do with anything?" he asked, perplexed by her sudden segue.

"Show, don't tell," Jaylah said, ignoring his question.

"Excuse me? I don't under—"

"No disrespect, Johnny, but at this point, your words don't mean shit. Don't get me wrong. They're nice to hear, and most times I believe them, but if they aren't backed by up by actions, then there're just meaningless words."

"Now, hold on just a minute. Where are we right now? Are we in England? Is this your flat?" Johnny looked around the hotel room, his voice rising. "No, we're in L.A. because *you* asked me to come. I got on a plane and flew 11 bloody hours—*in the middle seat,* by the way—because you asked me to come. "

"And I appreciate it, but—"

"But nothing, Jaylah. I *am* showing you with my actions. You asked me to move out of my house and now I'm living in a fucking hotel. You asked me to come, and I'm here. You asked me to meet your parents and I'm meeting them tonight. That's not enough action for you?"

"I appreciate those things, Johnny, I do. But now I'm asking you to tell your family I exist. That I matter," Jaylah said, her voice cracking. "That we're having a baby. That you want to be with me. That I didn't ruin your life."

He crossed the room and wrapped his arms around her waist and planted his lips on her forehead. "I will, Jaylah."

"When?" She glanced up at him, her eyes moist again. "When, Johnny? The time will never be right. It's not going to get any easier to tell them you and Fiona didn't work out, and that you fell in love with someone else."

Johnny collapsed on the bed and put his head in his hands. "I know," he whispered. "I just...I just don't like letting anyone down, especially my father. He expects so much of me. Sometimes it feels impossible to live up to it, innit?"

Something inside Jaylah softened. Seeing Johnny, *her Johnny*—who always seemed to move through the world like he owned it—humbled and vulnerable drew her closer to him. She sat in his lap and tipped his chin toward her face until they were looking into each other's eyes.

"I totally understand. I lived my whole life trying to measure up to everyone else's standards. And I was miserable. I felt like one of those lab rats suck in cage. Just trapped. But you know what happened when I broke out?" She stroked the side of his face and waited.

"Everything magically worked out?" A meager smile appeared on Johnny's lips.

"No, not everything. But I moved to London, got a wonderful job, and met this handsome bloke who I can't seem to get rid of no matter how hard I try," she said, smiling. "You know what I've learned over the years?"

Johnny shook his head.

"Whenever you take a risk things get rougher before they get better. But in the end, it's usually worth it."

"Really?" Johnny thought for a moment, and then kissed her, letting his tongue play gently in her mouth. "I hope you're right."

"I usually am," she teased, nuzzling his nose.

They cuddled for a few minutes, Johnny rubbing her back and nuzzling her neck, and Jaylah stroking his head. No matter how angry she had gotten with him minutes before, Jaylah was happy things were right between them once again.

Johnny broke their comfortable silence. "Can you hand me my phone?"

Jaylah reached across the bed, got Johnny's mobile, and handed it to him. "Who are you calling?"

"My father," he said, scrolling through his contacts.

Jaylah's heart leapt. *Is he...,* she thought, unable to allow herself to even think that Johnny was finally going to tell his family what they had was real and permanent and valuable.

"What are you going to say?"

He kissed her lips and pressed send. "What I should have said a long time ago."

Johnny put the phone on speaker and waited for his father to pick up.

"You don't have to...I don't need to hear—" Jaylah started to say, but Johnny waved her off and grabbed her hand. When she heard his father's voice boom into the receiver her stomach raced to her throat.

"Hello Papa, how are you?" Johnny asked as calmly as if he was just calling to shoot the breeze.

"Fine son. Are you well? How are things in England? How's the firm?"

"Things are well, Papa. Business is busy, but doing really well."

"Wonderful. Does this mean we'll be seeing you soon? You mother would love to have you home, she says you get too skinny when you stay in London too long."

Jaylah listened to the men's familiar banter and imagined what it would be like to travel to Accra and meet Johnny's family. She wondered if he got his striking looks from his father, or if he was, unlike her, his mother's child. She let herself daydream about helping Johnny's mother cook dinner as she balanced her little one on her hip while the men talked business in the other room. Jaylah could almost taste the Jollof Rice and barbequed goat when she felt Johnny squeeze her hand, causing her fantasy to drift away.

"Papa," she heard him say, his voice steady and assured, "I called because I have some news."

13

Love is a battle, Jaylah thought, as she looked at Johnny's slumped shoulders. He had put up a valiant effort against his father's assault on his manhood, on his intelligence, but Johnny appeared to be broken in a way Jaylah had never seen.

His conversation with the elder Poku had not gone well, although, Jaylah didn't expect Johnny's father to take the news of his son's affair, divorce, and unborn child kindly. But she couldn't predict Mr. Poku would go on such a tirade, calling Johnny stupid, worthless, and "an absolute failure of a man."

Jaylah winced when he'd levied that last blow, as if she had been the one sucker punched. And in a way she had. His father's attack on her lover's abilities had been as much about her as it was about Johnny's indiscretions.

"This girl," Johnny's father hissed, "is worth throwing away your life?"

"Her name is Jaylah," he said, correcting his father before giving an answer. "And yes, she is."

"How can you be so stupid? Fiona is a good woman, an elegant woman. You've known her since uni. And this, this girl comes along and now you want to mix up your life? Tuh!" Johnny's father boomed, his distaste for Jaylah evident in his refusal to use her name.

"Papa, Fiona and I haven't been happy for years. We haven't—"

"So what!" his father spat. "Marriage is not always happy, but you don't get divorced because of it. You had your fun, now go home to your wife."

"I'm in love with Jaylah, Papa. I want to be with her, she makes me happy."

"I understand this girl makes you feel things, but she's not worth ruining your life."

Jaylah's heart lurched. She wanted to defend herself, wanted to explain that she was, in fact, worth it. She wanted to tell Johnny's father that she loved his son with a fierceness that was so foreign, so against her character that it could not be explained away as some sort of fanciful whim that would soon pass.

"She didn't ruin my life. I did. I stayed with Fiona even though I knew marrying her was a mistake. I was drowning, Papa. Jaylah saved me, she brought me back to life."

"You are confused," Johnny's father said, ignoring his son's heartfelt words. "Come home, get your bearings straight, and patch things up with Fiona. She will take you back."

"Papa, my relationship with Fiona is finished. Done," Johnny said, slicing through the air with his hands as he spoke. "Jaylah and I are having a baby and we're going to get married."

Johnny's father sucked his teeth at the news of his impending grandchild. "I see this girl did not waste any time trapping you," he said, causing a new pang of anger to ricochet through Jaylah's limbs. She leapt up from the bed and mouthed the words *"trapped you?"* to Johnny, pissed off that the decision she agonized over had been reduced to a cheap trick by a conniving woman. "Offer her some money, son, and I'm sure she will go away. Then you can get back to your life."

Johnny blew out a rush of air, then reached out for Jaylah's hand. "Papa, she didn't trap me, and she's not going anywhere. We're getting married. I hope you and mum can support me on this."

"Support you?" Johnny's father laughed harshly. "I'm supposed to support my son's stupidity? I wouldn't dream of it. If you insist on ruining your life, I won't be apart of it."

Johnny looked at his phone in disbelief. "What are you saying?"

"Call me when you've come to your senses and are back home with your wife!" his father snapped before hanging up the phone, ruining their chance of a happy afternoon.

Jaylah searched her heart for the words that would soothe Johnny's wounds, but she doubted whatever she said could assuage the pain he felt from his father's rebuke. It was one thing for Johnny's father to blame her for ruining his son's life, but it was quite another to disown his only son because he disagreed with Johnny's choice.

The stakes had just been raised, and Jaylah knew that being kicked out of the Poku clan would either force them to grow closer together or pull them apart. At the moment, though, it was impossible to predict which would occur.

Jaylah walked up behind Johnny and put her hands around his waist. She rested her head on his back and inhaled his musky cologne. He leaned into her embrace, and for a moment, Jaylah felt like she was holding him up.

"I'm proud of you," she said after a few minutes. "And I love you."

Johnny turned to face her and kissed Jaylah on the lips. "Good. Because you and the baby are all I've got."

She probed his face for signs that he was joking, but found none. Johnny was right; she was it.

"But is that enough?"

Johnny tried to smile, but the feeling never reached his eyes. Jaylah wanted to cheer him up, but words continued to fail her. She felt like all the king's horses and all the king's men, hoping to piece her lover back together. Jaylah wanted him to be the sanguine man she'd fallen hard for and had given herself to without even thinking twice, but she just couldn't figure out what to say.

Jaylah found his lips again, drawing him into her and kissing him with a passion that startled them both. She grabbed his t-shirt and pulled it quickly over his head before running her tongue over his nipples.

He started to speak, "Jaylah...I'm not in the—" but she ignored his protest and continued nibbling her way down his chest to his stomach. She paused at his belly button and traced it with her tongue, then unbuckled his pants and slipped her hand in his boxers. She felt him swell at her touch and Johnny let out a sharp grunt when she began massaging him.

Jaylah may not have known what to say to coax Johnny back to himself, but she could show him that he wasn't stupid or worthless or foolish. She could remind him that she not only wanted him, but also needed him more than anyone else in the world.

Jaylah followed the tuffs of hair that ran from Johnny's stomach to the space between his thighs, smothering him in warm kisses before taking his shaft between her lips. She sucked him slowly, carefully, a thank you for he fighting for their love.

It was clear Johnny was his father's son—stubborn, resolute, not easily crushed—and longed for his approval. So the fact that he had not only gone to battle for her, but was willing to walk away from his family, confirmed what they had was stronger than either of them had ever imagined.

Johnny grabbed Jaylah's hair and thrust himself deeper into her mouth. She held onto his hips and listened as his sounds grew louder and less controlled. She wanted him to move insider her, closing the gap between them and once again fusing them into one body.

Jaylah pushed Johnny onto the bed and climbed on top of him, sliding down into his lap. They rocked together, matching each other's rhythm and refusing to rush to the end, even though they were both close to their peak. Johnny covered her mouth with his and allowed his tongue to play between her lips while his hips pushed deeper into her. Each time she drew him in, her muscles clinching, Johnny exhaled her name, nudging Jaylah closer and closer to surrendering to the force building in her loins.

"Don't leave me, Jaylah. Don't ever leave me," he said over and over again as he swam inside her dampness.

Jaylah vibrated as pressure rippled through her middle and out to her limbs. Johnny rolled her over, claiming the top spot so he could look in her eyes when she came. He stroked her harder, deeper, grunting promises to protect and love her forever.

"Please, please, please," he begged as he exploded inside her, "don't ever leave me, baby."

Johnny collapsed and rested his head in the crook of her neck while he caught his breath. Jaylah rubbed his back, trying to stop her heart from cracking open at the urgency in his words. Johnny had never had a problem expressing his love for her, but the pleading stunned her.

"Yes," Johnny said when he was able to speak.

"Yes, what?" Jaylah had no clue what Johnny was talking about, but would've granted him anything in that moment.

"You and the baby are enough. More than enough."

Jaylah's heart danced. It was official, they were a family. No matter who doubted it, they were a little three-person unit that she had stumbled on by accident, but would do anything to protect.

And at that moment Jaylah pitied anyone who dared get in their way.

14

"I was thinking," Jaylah said, watching Johnny get dressed for dinner. "Maybe I should change the date of my return ticket to London."

Johnny popped his head in the room, looking concerned. "You don't want to stay longer, do you? I don't think I could bear more than a few weeks of this."

"No, I mean, maybe I should just go..."

"Home?" he asked, finishing her sentence.

"Yeah. Since I'm not shipping my things and I've already cleaned out my old apartment, there's nothing left for me to do here. I don't really have a reason to stay."

He put on his tie. "What about your parents?"

"I think I've seen enough of them for a while," Jaylah snickered. "Besides, I need to get back to work before Hillary changes her mind about me. Then my ass will be deported. I don't want to press my luck, especially since I'll have to take a little time off for the baby."

"A little time off? You mean a few months, yeah?"

"No, I don't think I'll need that long. As long as everything goes well, I can go back to work a few weeks after having it."

Johnny looked at her for a moment, opened his mouth to speak, and then shook his head.

"What?"

"Nothing." Johnny looked himself over in the mirror before putting on his jacket.

"Mr. Poku, I know when you have something to say. Out with it."

He hesitated. "It's just....I don't think you should be in such a rush to get back to work after the baby is born."

She rolled her eyes. *This conversation. Again.*

"I'm not going to give up my job, Johnny. You know I'm not the stay at home type. I love writing, and if you want me to quit, then we're going to have a *huge* problem."

He crossed the room and stood in front of her. "I'm not suggesting you give up writing."

"So what *are* you saying then?" she asked, hands on her hips.

Johnny put his arms around her waist and pulled her closer to him. "Just keep an open mind. Things might change. You may need, or want, to take time off. And that's okay. You don't have to try to be superwoman. You're not in this alone, Jaylah. Remember that."

"No, *you* remember that when the baby is screaming its head off at three in the morning and I don't feel like getting up."

Johnny grinned. "I'll try."

He leaned down and kissed her, his hands tracing her breasts through the fabric of her dress.

"Don't get fresh, Mr. Poku." Jaylah moved them back to her waist. "My parents are expecting us."

"We can be a few minutes late, innit."

"Not if you want my mother to like you," she said, straightening his tie.

"Well, we can't have both sets of parents hating me, can we?" he said, trying to make a joke but Jaylah could tell the wound from his father's admonishment was still tender.

"I'm sorry, for—"

"It's not your fault," he said, cutting her off. "My father is a very obstinate man, especially when he thinks you've made a bad choice."

Even though Johnny had stuck up for her, his words still stung. *A bad choice.* Did Johnny make a bad choice when he fell in love with Jaylah? Despite what he said, would he come to view her as a grand mistake that had started his life downhill?

Jaylah's mind began to spin, causing her to stumble away from Johnny. He caught her hand and brought her back to his chest.

"But I have no doubt," he said, looking directly in her eyes. "You're the best choice I've made in years, Jaylah. *Years.*"

Johnny opened the door, then stepped aside to let her pass through. "I mean, just look at that ass." He pinched her butt as she walked through the door. "That alone is worth it."

As they set out to meet her parents, Jaylah prayed he was right. Everything they'd been through, and had still yet to experience, would hopefully be worth it.

⬥

"Mom, dad, this is Jonathan Poku," Jaylah said, finally introducing her parents to the man she loved. "Johnny, these are my parents, Sarah and Joe Baldwin."

"It's a pleasure to meet you Mr. and Mrs. Baldwin," Johnny said, leaning in to greet them.

"Please, call me Joe," Mr. Baldwin said, clapping Johnny on the back as the men shook hands.

Jaylah kept her gaze on her mother and tried to read her thoughts, but in these situations—welcoming someone to her home—Mrs. Baldwin rarely let her true feelings escape. Ever the perfect hostess, Mrs. Baldwin kept her smile light and her tone charming.

"Johnny, we're happy to have you. We've heard so much about you." She looked at her daughter and winked. "Can I take your jacket and get you a drink? We've got water, pop, wine..."

"...And beer," Mr. Baldwin broke in before asking his wife, "Honey, can you grab me one?" He motioned toward Johnny, "What do you say, Jonathan? Want to share a cold one while the ladies gossip about us?"

Johnny laughed politely. "Sure, Sir, that would be fine."

"Joe," Mr. Baldwin corrected, "call me Joe, son."

"Okay, as long as you call me Johnny."

"You got it!"

Mr. Baldwin sat off toward the den, and Johnny quickly kissed Jaylah on the side of her head before following after him. When the men were out of earshot, Mrs. Baldwin spoke up.

"Well..." she gushed, "isn't he just gorgeous." Jaylah grinned; her mother was never shy about noticing, and commenting on, handsome men. Whenever they'd go to brunch Mrs. Baldwin would always point out good-looking waiters or diners. *"You're married!"* Jaylah would tell her mother, playfully rolling her eyes. *"Yes, and I haven't gone blind yet,"* Mrs. Baldwin would always answer.

"Help me with the drinks Jay Jay."

Jaylah trailed behind her mother, catching a glimpse of her father and Johnny. They seemed to be getting on well, both men smiling and animated as they talked.

When they got into the expansive kitchen Jaylah grabbed two beers from the fridge and popped them open, then pulled out a bottle of San Pellegrino for herself and her mother.

"Want me to take these out now?"

"No, we'll let them talk for a bit. You know how your father is; he's probably already going on about the Lakers or something. Besides, it'll give us a little time to catch up," Mrs. Baldwin said, no doubt relishing the idea of a chinwag with her daughter.

Jaylah knew "catch up" actually meant interrogate and her stomach immediately flip-flopped. She wanted to grab the bottle of merlot that was resting in the wine cooler and pour herself a large glass, but she resisted. Jaylah didn't need both Johnny and her mother getting on her case for having a glass of vino tonight. Instead, she cracked open the San Pellegrino and squeezed a generous amount of lime juice into the sparkling water, and took a sip to calm her nerves.

"Johnny has on a lovely suit tonight. What is that? Ralph Lauren?" she asked, placing the hors d'oeuvres on a sterling silver tray.

"Zegna, I think. He got it yesterday."

"Yesterday? That must've cost him a pretty penny."

"Yeah, nearly $2500," she said; her mother's eyes widened. "I know."

"Hmph," Mrs. Baldwin hummed. "So he does well for himself?"

"Let's put it this way, he's not worried about paying the rent," Jaylah chuckled. "He does okay, I guess."

"You're not sure? You have to be sure, Jay Jay. You're having a baby with this man."

Jaylah resisted the impulse to roll her eyes. She knew her mother only wanted the best for her, but lately, every time they spoke she felt like Mrs. Baldwin had forgotten she was actually an adult who no longer needed her lectures.

"I'm pretty sure, mother. He drives a Benz, owns a townhouse, and works in finance. He's certainly better off than I am."

"Cars and houses don't mean a thing, Jay Jay." Mrs. Baldwin shook her head like her daughter had completely missed the point. "You need to know he can take care of you. Now grab those drinks."

Jaylah and her mother filed out of the kitchen looking like two distant branches of a family tree. Mrs. Baldwin: slim, petite, and the color of cafe au lait. Jaylah: tall, voluptuous, and skin the hue of red clay after it rains. The only thing they seemed to have in common was their hair—thick, curly, and downright unruly at times. Mrs. Baldwin trimmed hers into a neat afro, while Jaylah let her tresses run wild atop her head. The mismatched pair interrupted the men just as they were debating which was the more difficult sport, soccer or basketball.

"Johnny, I hope you brought your appetite," Mrs. Baldwin said, placing a tray of salmon croquettes between the men. "You do eat fish, right dear?"

"I eat anything, ma'am," Johnny said, giving Mrs. Baldwin an easy smile.

"Great! Dinner will be ready shortly, but these should tide you over." She motioned toward Jaylah who handed each man a beer. "Need anything else fellas?"

Mr. Baldwin shook his head as he stuffed a croquette in his mouth. "No, ma'am, I'm fine, thank you," Johnny spoke up for the both of them.

"Wonderful!" She clapped her hands and Jaylah marveled at her mother's hosting skills. "Jay Jay, will you help me in the kitchen?"

Jaylah gave Johnny a look that seemed to say, *help,* and he reached out and quickly squeezed her hand. He knew she was dreading the evening, and Jaylah interpreted his tiny gesture as confirmation that everything might just be okay.

She returned to the kitchen to help her mother, but soon realized that Mrs. Baldwin, as usual, had everything under control.

"Like I was saying," her mother said, picking up their conversation right where they left off, "you need to be certain Johnny can take care of you and the baby, Jay Jay. Otherwise, the prudent thing to do is stay right here where your father and I can help out."

"I can take care of myself, mother. I have a job, you know."

"I know, sweetie, and I'm proud of you. I certainly wouldn't have had the gumption to pick up and move to another country. A shopping trip? Yes. But move?" Mrs. Baldwin kissed her teeth, and Jaylah was surprised her mother was actually proud she had taken a risk. Usually Mrs. Baldwin's praise was reserved for achievements—doing well in school, writing a cover story for the paper. Jaylah's mother rarely gave her props for doing something courageous, especially when she didn't agree with the decision.

Mrs. Baldwin walked around the granite island and stared up into her daughter's face.

"Jay Jay, I know you can take care of yourself, but you're bringing a new life into the world. You need to be certain you can count on this man and he can take care of you if, God forbid, something goes wrong," she patted her daughter's hand. "How do you know he's not just showing off? Johnny could be in financial trouble or mired in debt and you could end up supporting *him*." Mrs. Baldwin made a face like she smelled something sour. "Can you imagine?"

Supporting him? The mere thought of it sounded utterly ridiculous. Johnny would certainly not let that happen, he was too proud. The need to defend her man arose in Jaylah. Even if they lost it all, they could still make it, she figured. Money wasn't everything; her parents had proved that.

"Firstly, Johnny would *never* let me support him. *Ever*," Jaylah told her mother. "And anyway, you and daddy didn't have a lot of money when you first got married. Now look at you. Things worked out."

"Your father and I have known each other forever. We grew up together, remember? I know Joe better than he knows himself. Can you say the same for Johnny?"

The question caught Jaylah off guard. Going in to dinner she predicted her traditional, Southern mother would all but push her into a quickie marriage with the father of her unborn child. After all, isn't that what her parents had done? But here Mrs. Baldwin was trying to make sure Johnny was worthy of *her*. The conversation was both perplexing and a pleasant surprise.

Jaylah was sure she loved Johnny, she was sure she was having their child, but beyond that? She couldn't say.

Jaylah had to admit her mother was right. They didn't know each other well enough to even consider forever just yet, not with so much unfinished business left to tie up.

"We're in no rush, mom. Well..." Jaylah hesitated, "Well, I'm not, at least. He wants to get married, you know, do the honorable thing? But I'm just not sure."

Jaylah was surprised she was being so candid with her mom. She'd spent her entire life editing down her thoughts to the answers she felt her mother would find most acceptable. But the jig was up. If Jaylah couldn't woman up and be frank with her mother at damn near 30, and while carrying her own child, maybe she wasn't ready for this whole ordeal in the first place.

"If it were up to him, we'd be married, I'd be at home with my feet up, and he'd be taking care of everything," Jaylah said, rolling her eyes.

Her mother chuckled. "What's wrong with that?"

"Everything. Absolutely everything," Jaylah said. "I love Johnny, and this whole having a baby thing caught me completely flatfooted, but I'm dealing with it. I just won't let this baby slow me down, mom. I have things I want to accomplish, you know?"

"Like your book?"

"That's one of them. I just..." Jaylah threw her hands up like she was hoping the right words would fall into her palms. "I just don't want to look back and think, 'I fucked up my life.'" Mrs. Baldwin raised her eyebrow, but didn't correct her daughter's language. "Sorry, but you know what I mean."

"I do, which is why I'm concerned. You could move home and we can..."

"I can't!" Jaylah cut in, her tone more biting than she wanted it to be. "Mom, I love you and daddy, but I can't move home. I've gotta make my own way, you know? That's one reason I love London so much. It's the first time I made a choice on my own...because I wanted to. Not because it was the right thing to do, and not because it was what you and daddy wanted. It was *MY* choice."

Jaylah eyed her mother and waited to be reprimanded, but Mrs. Baldwin remained silent and let her daughter speak.

"I know you guys want the best for me, but it's time you just let me make my own decisions. If I mess up, I mess up. But you and daddy can't protect me from living. I have to do that on my own. Don't worry, you raised me right," Jaylah said, staring down into her mother's flawless face. She cracked a wry smile. "Well...except I did get knocked up. But I hear that's sort of a family tradition."

Mrs. Baldwin's eyes fluttered wide, then she broke out in a big grin. "I'm going to kill your father!" she said, laughing. "I didn't want you to struggle like we did, Jay Jay. I wasn't ready to be a mother when you came along. I just wanted you have an easier life than I did."

"But you made it, mom."

"We did, but we struggled for a long while. Your father worked two jobs after we graduated, sometimes three, just so I could stay home with you. And even then, times were tough."

"Yet you guys pulled through. You raised an amazing daughter," Jaylah chuckled, "And you ended up having a great life, right?"

"Yes, yes we did," Mrs. Baldwin admitted. "Heck, we still do!"

"Exactly. Let me have that mom. Let me live the way I see fit without you and daddy swooping in to protect me like I'm back in elementary school and skinned my knee."

Jaylah's eyes brimmed with tears, but this time they were happy ones. She couldn't remember a time when she and her mother spoke as equals, just two women sharing their hopes, dreams, and stories. She hugged her mother and began to regret the attitude she'd served up since she'd been home. Sure, Jaylah was going through some things, but her mother only wanted her to be happy and protected. Why was it so difficult for Jaylah to see that before?

"It won't be easy," Mrs. Baldwin said, wiping a tear from her daughter's cheek. "And I'm not going to hold my tongue. But I know you can make your own decisions, Jay Jay. You're stronger than you think, sweetie. And we support you no matter what."

"Thank you, mommy," Jaylah said, reverting back to her younger self, just for a moment. "Thank you...for everything."

"It's what mother's do. You'll learn," she said, patting her daughter's stomach.

The women hugged again and Jaylah luxuriated in her mother's comforting embrace. It had been so long since she felt totally accepted by her mother, but maybe she had been wrong about her the whole time. Maybe Jaylah already had her mother's approval and didn't even realize it.

Had she been fighting against a force that hadn't even been there all along?

"Mom, I'm..."

Mrs. Baldwin held up her hand and halted her daughter mid-sentence. "No apologies necessary, Jay Jay. None of us have ever been here before and we're all doing the best we can," she said, rubbing her daughter's back. "Just keep your eyes open and listen to your gut, hear me?"

Jaylah nodded.

"I can tell Johnny cares for you, and it's easy to get caught up in how beautiful he is. I mean, that suit alone is pretty distracting, isn't it?" Mrs. Baldwin grinned.

Jaylah shrugged her shoulders. "He wanted to make a good impression."

"Well, it'll take a lot more than an expensive suit," Mrs. Baldwin chuckled before turning serious. "Everything beautiful ain't good for you, sweetie, look at oleanders. It's okay to admire how great they look, but get too close and they can wreak havoc on your system."

"Is this some sort of down home, Bayou country wisdom? Did Grand'Mere give you this same speech?" Jaylah tried to dampen the impact of her mother's words with a joke.

"Laugh if you want to, but you need to figure out which one Johnny is for you, sweetie. Is he an oleander or Echinacea? One can literally kill you, while the other gives you life," Mrs. Baldwin said, her tone hinting that she was ready to see what her daughter's lover was all about. She grabbed a crystal platter and motioned for her daughter to follow her lead. "C'mon, Jay Jay. I know I'm ready to find out."

15

Finally. Jaylah exhaled as she gazed out of the airplane window somewhere over the Atlantic. She was on her way home after what felt like an eternity in Los Angeles. Although she dreaded the trip to California, Jaylah had to admit things went better than expected. After her parents got over the initial shock of her pregnancy, she was able to settle her affairs and escape with her sanity in tact. A serious coup.

To Jaylah's surprise, dinner with her parents had gone off without a hitch, and the conversation with her mother reminded her that she was a grown woman who was smart enough to make up her own mind based on her own needs, not anyone else's.

Looking back, Jaylah was shocked she had been the one to broach the subject of marriage, not her parents. Instead, Sarah and Joe appeared content to fill Johnny in on her life before they met, sticking in stories that made him howl with laughter, like the one about her brief bout of vegetarianism at nine.

After watching a baby calf being born during a field trip to a local farm, Jaylah informed her parents she would no longer eat meat and would live on chocolate chip cookies for the rest of her life.

"It lasted an hour," Mr. Baldwin said, shaking his head. "When Sarah fixed dinner and Jay Jay realized all she could eat was okra, it was over. She was back on animals before the plates cleared!"

Johnny seemed to love hearing about Jaylah's life. He sat next to her gazing at her parents with what could only be described as reverence. She wondered if he was really enamored with her family or if he was missing his own. They were having such a good time she didn't want to mess it up with a misplaced question, so Jaylah let it go. Still, it dogged her.

"Feeling homesick already?" Johnny asked, sitting next to her on the plane.

"For L.A.? Not at all." She chuckled. "I'm ready to get back to my life. Just thinking, that's all."

"About?"

"Things," she said, in no rush to fill in the blanks. Johnny didn't press her for an answer and she let the silence multiple between them.

"Dinner went better than I expected," she admitted when she was ready to talk. Jaylah kept her gazed trained on the dark ocean outside her window. "I mean, my parents didn't even press us about getting married. I guess I was totally off base with that one."

"Your father and I had a talk," Johnny said so casually she almost missed it.

"Wait. What? What kind of talk? When?"

"When you and your mum were in the kitchen dishing up the food."

Jaylah scoured her memory to see if she missed anything about that night. She and her mother had their own heart-to-heart, but it didn't seem to last long enough for her father to grill Johnny about their future. Besides, Mr. Baldwin had seemed like his usual jovial self that evening, calling Johnny "son" and discussing sports. When had they had this talk? And what had been said?

"We were only gone a few minutes, what could you have possibly talked about?"

"Things," Johnny said, mimicking her tone with a smile.

"C'mon Johnny, what did he say?"

"Well, he didn't mince any words. He wanted to know if I loved you..."

"And what did you say?" Jaylah asked, butting in.

Johnny scrunched up his face and looked at her like she'd gone mad. "What do you think I said? No?"

"Whatever. What else? Did you tell him about your divorce?"

"No, that didn't come up. We just talked," Johnny said, shrugging. "You know how men are. Your father informed me he'd kick my ass if I 'messed you over. He also wanted to know what I did for a living and if I was prepared to support you and the baby."

Jaylah relaxed; if anything had gone wrong she would have heard about it before she left. He mother would certainly tell her if her father disapproved of Johnny or had concerns about their conversation.

After that night, Jaylah spent the next two days waiting to hear something, anything, negative about Johnny from her parents, but they never uttered a word. As a matter of fact, her father had called him a "fine young man" and they'd even gone to play golf the following day. In retrospect, Jaylah was stunned things had run as smoothly as they had.

"Once I assured him I was not only excited about being a father, but also more than capable of providing for you and the baby, he seemed satisfied. I didn't have to show him any financial statements or any-thing," Johnny chuckled, "but I think I was able to put his concerns to rest."

Jaylah leaned back in her seat and closed her eyes. "Well, that's a relief."

"Oh, and we talked about this."

Johnny took a small teal box out of his pocket and placed it on the tray in front of her. He peered at Jaylah, a smile beaming from his lips. She eyed the box, saw TIFFANY & CO stamped across the cover, and suddenly lost the ability to speak.

Even though she'd run this scenario through her head a million times Jaylah wasn't ready for a proposal. Not now. Not when she'd all but told herself that getting engaged to Johnny when everything in their lives seemed so up in the air was the worst idea ever.

Despite knowing Johnny wanted to get married, and hearing him tell his father they were going to tie the knot as if it was an indisputable fact, Jaylah was still caught off guard by the little aquamarine box.

If Jaylah had been standing she would have fallen down, bowled over by the gravity of the moment, but she was sitting, and he was looking at her expectantly.

"Wha...what...what is that?" she stuttered, eye-balling the box.

"Why don't you open it and see."

"I don't under..." she stammered. "When did you get this?"

"The day I went out with your father," he said, still smiling.

"My dad knows about this? He's okay with it? How come he didn't tell me?" she was asking herself and Johnny at once.

"I wanted it to be a surprise. Open it."

Jaylah gaped at Johnny still unable to comprehend the moment. He nodded slightly, encouraging her to open the box. Her fingers crept toward the ribbon, but quickly recoiled when she touched it like she'd been shocked.

Johnny laughed. "It won't bite you, babes. I promise."

"My hands won't stop shaking," she said, as she removed the white bow. Jaylah paused and ran her fingers across the top of the small square box that held the promise of their future.

"Go on," he said, goading her to open the package that was no bigger than her palm.

Jaylah opened it and her breath hinging in her throat. "Ohmygod," she croaked, before looking at him, tears already flooding the corner of her eyes. "This is...this has to be too much."

The ring did not look real.

How could it possibly be real?

A large cushion-cut diamond rested atop a gleaming platinum band that was also rimmed in sparkling diamonds. The ring glistened under the jet's demure cabin lights, and Jaylah thought it looked like something Richard Burton might have given Elizabeth Taylor the first time around. Only smaller, of course, but no less brilliant.

This can't be for me.

Jaylah was unable to speak, blinded by luminous stones and rendered mute by the drumming of her heart. She blinked rapidly and tried to concentrate on breathing.

"Jaylah," Johnny said, snapping her back to the present and taking the ring out of the box. "I love you, babes. Neither one of us ever expected this, but here we are," he grinned, his own eyes moist. "But I can't imagine my life without you in it. I know we have some challenges ahead, but as long as you're by my side, I can deal with anything."

This has to be a dream. This isn't happening.

Jaylah attempted to focus on Johnny's words, but nothing about the scene seemed real. Her married boyfriend was proposing on a plane with a ring that looked like it had been ripped off a film star.

Fucking surreal, was all she could think. Nothing else made sense.

"I was going to set up a proper proposal, you know, at a restaurant or someplace really lovely," Johnny continued, leaning in close to Jaylah. "But I couldn't wait any longer. I don't want another day to go by without being certain you'll be mine. Forever."

Jaylah held her breath and tried to will herself to calm down, but everything in her body was set alight by his words.

"Jaylah Nicole Baldwin," Johnny said, grabbing her hand, "will you marry me? Please?"

Jaylah tried to speak, but the words jumbled on the tip of her tongue and all that made it past her lips was the sound of her tears.

"I...ohmygod, ohymygod, Johnny..." she said over and over, as he slipped the ring on her finger and kissed her lips, stopping the babbling, but not her crying.

"You've made me the happiest man in the fucking world, Jaylah," he said, wiping her face and kissing her again. "I love you so damn much, girl."

Johnny's words made her tingle, feeling every emotion, every teardrop, every beat of her heart at once. Jaylah longed to know how he'd pulled this off, how he could afford such an extravagant ring, and what he planned to do about his parents, but instead she melted into his arms and tried to commit the entire moment to memory.

Even before this Jaylah would have gladly done just about anything to make Johnny happy as long as it meant he would return her love in kind.

But as his mouth swept across every part of her exposed skin, there was one thing she just couldn't bring herself to say.

16

Jaylah walked into Barnyard and immediately spotted her sister sitting at a wooden table that looked like it had been torn off the frame of an old farmhouse. Clad in a black and white Aztec print skirt and red blouse, Jourdan was sipping a drink and scanning the menu when she saw Jaylah coming her way.

"Hey sissy!" she said, face breaking into a gigantic smile. "Well, you don't look fat!"

"Umm, I missed you too," Jaylah said, kissing Jourdan on the cheek. "Thanks for meeting me for lunch. I know you're in the middle of pulling the gallery opening together."

"Are you kidding? I would've run out and met the plane last night, but you were with *him*. I can't believe you were only gone a month. Felt like an entire year! How are the parents?"

"They're fine. Excited about everything."

"You owe me a drink, you know," Jourdan said. "After I finish this one, of course, and make it a double."

"For what?"

"You didn't believe me when I said you were keeping the baby. I knew you'd come 'round!"

Jaylah rolled her eyes and removed her coat, happy to be hanging with her girl once again. "Whatever."

"Admit it. You know I was right," she said, grinning at Jaylah. "Now for the details! How far along are you and what are we having?"

"Ten weeks, and currently a blob," Jaylah said, grabbing Jourdan's menu and eyeing her drink. "What is that? Rum?"

"Close, whiskey."

"I'm so jealous. I *really* want a drink right now."

"Let's make a deal. You eat for two and I'll drink for three. Okay?" Joudan said, draining the glass. "Now, let's give the blob a name! ..." She tapped her pale chin like she was deep in thought. "I know, we'll call it Nemo!"

Jaylah looked dumbfounded. "Like the cartoon?"

"Yes! Remember? 'Just keep swimming, just keep swimming.' That's what Nemo is doing, yeah?"

"Umm, that was Dory, J," Jaylah said, scrunching up her face.

"So! Nemo sounds a million times cuter than Dory. Dory sounds like some kind of disease you catch when you're bored. Anyway, hello little Nemo, it's your auntie speaking," Jourdan sang while Jaylah chuckled in spite of herself. She missed her friend's crazy antics, which always seemed to bring out the best in Jaylah.

When she first got to London Jourdan helped save her. Without introducing herself to the quirky blonde girl in the impossibly high boots Jaylah may have missed out on this part of her life all together.

After all, it was Jourdan who hooked her up with her *Glamour* editor, dragged her to the Mau Mau bar where she met Johnny, and folded Jaylah into her life so completely most people thought they were actually related. Since the moment they met, Jaylah felt blessed to have Jourdan in her life.

"So how did meeting the parents go? Did they warm to Johnny?" Jourdan asked, stuffing a piece of bread in her mouth and Jaylah took a long heavy sigh, like she was preparing to spill all of the gory details. "That well, huh?" Jourdan said. "Well, if it's any consolation, I happen to like the bloke."

"He proposed," Jaylah blurted, unable to contain the news any longer.

"Proposed...marriage?"

"Yes!" Jaylah screeched.

"With your parents looking on? That takes some balls."

"No, no. On the plane. On the way back here."

Jourdan grabbed Jaylah's hands and inspected her fingers for evidence of a proposal. "No ring? Isn't he some sort of a banker? He couldn't even give you a—" Jaylah pulled the teal box out of her purse and set it on the table bringing her friend's rant to a halt. Jourdan tore open the lid and gasped. "No fucking way!"

"I know…"

"You've got to be fucking kidding me. This ring is like…it looks like it cost a million pounds!"

Jaylah laughed. "I don't think it's quite that much, but it's crazy, right?"

"Why isn't it on your finger? I'd wear this rock *everywhere*, shoving it in everyone's face like, oh look, my ring costs more than your car." The women giggled as Jourdan wiggled her fingers in the air like she was the Queen waving to her loyal subjects. "But seriously, why aren't you wearing it? You would have to cut it off my cold, dead finger." Jourdan suddenly paused and eyed her friend, "Wait. Did you say no?"

"That's the thing," Jaylah said, lowering her voice and leaning in like she was about to tell Jourdan a secret, "I didn't say anything."

Her friend looked bewildered. "I don't understand. How can a man ask you to marry him, give you this *fabulous* ring, and you not say anything?"

"He didn't really give me a chance. After he was done with the speech he just slipped it on my finger and kissed me. I guess he just assumed I'd say yes."

"Like I said, he has balls, Jay." Jourdan admired the ring one final time before putting it back in the box. "So what are you going to do?"

"Wait till he brings it up again?"

Jourdan looked at her friend like she'd grown a pair of horns. "You can't be serious. You have to give him a proper answer. You have to straighten this out."

"That's the thing. I'm not sure what I want to do."

"You love him, yeah?"

"I do, but is that enough? Just because you love someone doesn't mean you should speed off and get married."

Jourdan raised her glass. "Here, here."

"Everything is already moving so fast. When you think about it, we really just met. Yeah, we messed up and I got pregnant, but I just want to catch my breath and really think things through before I make that kind of commitment."

"Sounds like you two need to have a conversation, sissy," Jourdan said, patting her friend's hand. "But whatever you do, keep the ring. It can make for one hell of a rainy day fund."

"See, this is why I love you. Always thinking ahead."

"Damn straight. Now that you're all hopped up on baby hormones one of us has to be the brains of this operation. You're lucky to have me."

"You know what, J? You're goddamn right."

Jaylah barely had time to breathe since returning to London. As soon as she hit the ground, she threw herself into work, covering musicians at the London Jazz Festival, taking in the explosion of fireworks for Guy Fawkes' Night, interviewing local chefs for her new series on the city's diverse food scene, and penning columns about being a new transport to the Queen's city. Jaylah tried to keep busy, never idling around the house or wandering the streets like she used to for fear her mind would linger too long on Johnny's proposal and what she should do about it.

Somehow, Jaylah had managed to avoid that conversation for weeks. After all, it wasn't like Johnny could press her to pick a wedding date or decide on a venue because he was still married and going through a divorce. Plus, like Jaylah, Johnny worked even longer hours since returning to London, dragging home well past nine each night chatting about brokering deals that could help them buy a house "in cash," he said one evening, "just from my commission alone."

These days, Johnny seemed preoccupied with talking about money more than usual. Previously, Jaylah never cared about his finances, but she guessed he was doing just fine. Between his car, home, the expensive gifts he gave her, and the fact that she never needed to pay for anything when they were together (and sometimes when they weren't), Jaylah never gave Johnny's finances any serious thought. But with her mother's advice—*be sure he can take care of you*—still ringing in her ears, Jaylah actually listened whenever he brought up money.

"I'm going to be home a little later than I planned tonight," Johnny said as Jaylah wrestled with a story she was working on at the dining table. He was gobbling up the last of the eggs and toast she fixed for him before he ran off to work.

"Again? I thought you were done with that project?"

"I am. I'm meeting with my solicitor after work," he said, draining his coffee in one large gulp.

She glanced up. "Everything alright?"

"Yeah..." he hesitated, seeming to weigh his words. "Fiona filed her own divorce petition. We're meeting to discuss it."

"What does that mean? Is she fighting it? I thought you said wanted to get divorced as well."

"She does. She she's just filing her own petition under different grounds."

"Which mean what exactly? What *grounds* is she using?" Jaylah asked, cutting him off.

"Adultery," he said quickly, sending a pang of guilt down Jaylah's spine.

"Adultery," she repeated quietly, her eyes instantly filling with water.

Johnny walked around the table to comfort her; he was never any match for her tears. "Shhh. Don't do that, please? It changes nothing, I promise. My solicitor thinks it's just her way of negotiating."

The words *home wrecker,* flashed before her eyes, once again making Jaylah feel like she'd destroyed Fiona's life. Despite telling herself a million times that Johnny had ruined his own marriage—that it was *his* choice, not hers—Jaylah couldn't help but feel like she and the baby had put the final nail in its coffin.

"Hey," he said, trying to coax her away from the sickening feeling that she'd shattered another woman's world. "Why don't you come with me? We can have dinner at after the meeting, yeah? We'll go someplace really lovely."

Jaylah shook her head and willed her emotions into check. "We're supposed to go to that gallery opening tonight, remember? I promised Jourdan we'd come. She's been working on it for months and this is a huge deal for her company. I have to be there."

"Shit, I totally forgot," he said, kneeling in front of her like he was getting ready to propose again. "Let me cancel the meeting with the solicitor then. What time's the opening?"

"Seven, but don't cancel it. You go to the meeting and get that sorted out. I'll go hang with Jourdan. Maybe we can all have dinner afterward."

"You sure? I can make another..." Jaylah put a finger to Johnny's lips, silencing him. Then she caressed the side of his smooth face. The truth was she wanted to hang with Jourdan alone. Every moment she and Johnny were together Jaylah was afraid he would bring up their engagement, and although she adored him, there were other things Jaylah felt she needed to focus on first before committing to be Johnny's *second* wife.

"Okay babes," he said, kissing her palm and noticing her naked ring finger. He scrunched up his face. "Where's your ring?"

She froze. It was still in her purse where it had been for the past few weeks. "I put it back in the box," she said slowly.

Johnny looked puzzled. "In the box? Why?"

Jaylah had a choice. She could either come clean about her ambivalence about their engagement or she could conjure up a lie.

"I..." She started to speak the truth, but changed her mind when they locked eyes. "My hands were swelling, so I took it off. I didn't want it to get stuck. I guess I need to drink more water or something." She shrugged, hoping he'd believe her.

"Oh..." Johnny seemed to run her answer through his head. "Do you need me to go to the store to grab some water or ginger ale before I leave? I don't want you to get dehydrated again."

She kissed his lips. "No I'm fine. I can't drink water on an empty stomach anyway or it'll come back up."

"Then eat something. How come you didn't make yourself any eggs?"

"I will, babe. Eating makes me sleepy and I want to finish this first," she said, trying to smile wide enough to put him at ease.

"Okay. I'll call you later, yeah? If you feel up to it, maybe we can meet for lunch."

"Sounds good."

She walked him to the door and met his lips.

"Jaylah? Please drink water, okay? You have to get that ring back on. I don't want guys out here getting their hopes up," he said, smiling. "You're already taken."

Victoria Miro's Hackney gallery was abuzz with art lovers from every corner of the city. Expansive, colorful canvases, gritty photographs, and intricately woven tapestries clung to the stark white walls, and from the looks of things, the well-heeled hipsters seemed to eat it all up.

Jaylah moved through the space looking for Jourdan and trying to decide on whether or not she'd finally have a glass of wine. Although she'd Googled "wine + pregnancy" several times trying to be sure that an occasional glass wouldn't harm the baby, she hadn't decided if she would actually take the plunge.

Walking through the gallery Jaylah admired Jourdan's work. Her friend's PR firm had spearheaded this year's 30 Under 30 opening, showcasing the most promising emerging artists in the city and connecting them with the people who could be the difference between giving up their passion to get a day job, or being a world-renowned artist.

For months Jourdan vented about the difficulty of putting on such a show and how some of the more pretentious assholes, as she called them, took longer to confirm they would attend. But gazing out over the crowd it was clear Jourdan had pulled it off, and hopefully, it meant the tiny PR firm she'd started after dropping out of university at 21 to throw parties could finally spread its wings and fly.

"You did it, J," Jaylah said, looping an arm around Jourdan's waist, startling her friend. "This looks amazing!"

Jourdan hugged Jaylah and grinned. "Can you believe it? I thought it would never come together!"

"But it did!" Jaylah said, letting her eyes travel around the room again.

"I'm such a bloody mess, though. I need a drink to calm me down. My heart is pounding like I just ran a fucking marathon and you *know* I don't run!"

Jaylah laughed and shook her head. "Girl, me either. I believe a toast is in order. Let's get you a drink."

The pair walked toward the bar, which was situated along a wall of windows overlooking Wharf Road. Seeing her friend dressed in a chic paisley print jumpsuit, black blazer, and red heels made Jaylah feel underdressed. She'd planned on wearing the Duro Olow pencil skirt Johnny had bought her a few months ago and burgundy blouse, but she couldn't zip it up. Jaylah was forced to settle on a black shift dress that made her feel like a cow and a pair of nude wedges instead.

"What would you like to drink?" the bartender asked them when they made it to the front of the line.

"Two glasses of champagne, please," Jourdan said before Jaylah had a chance to speak up. "The good stuff from the bottom shelf. And don't be stingy,"

Jaylah cocked an eyebrow at her friend. "It's a celebration. I won't let you make it a habit, and I won't let anything happen to Nemo on my watch."

When Jaylah got her glass she inhaled deeply, letting the bubbles tickle her nose before taking a tiny sip, hoping to stretch the decadent glass out for as a long as possible.

"So where's the boy. Working late?" Jourdan asked after taking a gulp of her champagne.

"No, meeting with his solicitor. He might meet us later for dinner if you're up to it."

"Everything alright?"

Jaylah shrugged. "He says so, but I'm not sure. Fiona filed her own divorce petition. She's suing him for adultery."

Jourdan's eyes went wide. "What?"

"Exactly. When he filed the papers he chose 'unreasonable behavior' as the grounds because he said it was the easiest, less messy option."

"Right, so I've heard. But she doesn't want to go along with it?"

"I guess not. His solicitor thinks it's just a negotiation tactic. Maybe she's just trying to protect herself. I can't really blame her. I mean, if I were in her shoes I'd probably do the same thing."

Jourdan nodded in agreement, but her head suddenly snapped up. "Wait. Is she naming you?"

"Naming me in what?"

"Her petition. That's an option, you know, especially if you claim adultery. You can name the other person and they get pulled into the proceedings."

"You're fucking kidding me," Jaylah said in disbelief.

Naming me? Would Fiona do that?

"Not at all. Happened to a mate of mine. He had an affair with this older woman, I didn't quite get it, but whatever. Anyway, when the husband found out, he divorced his wife and named my mate in the petition. He had to go to court and everything."

Jourdan's words crashed into Jaylah like a hurricane, threatening to knock her off balance. Would Fiona actually sue *her* for adultery? And what would that even mean? Could it mess with her immigration status? Would the UK suddenly find her unworthy of a Visa because she was amoral?

Jaylah resisted the urge to bolt out of the gallery and find Johnny to get some answers. She could deal with helping him through the divorce, but she absolutely did not want her name sullied by Johnny and Fiona's relationship drama. He said it himself; this was not her fault. But why did it always feel like it was?

"Be right back, Jay. I need to go chat with that bloke over there. He owns a galley in Mayfair. *A big one.* Maybe I can convince him to come on as a client."

Jaylah could do little more than nod. All of the excitement she just had was zapped away by the thought of being branded an adulterer *in court*. Jaylah couldn't give Jourdan her typical "go get him girl!" pep talk right now, not that her friend needed it anyway.

She fumbled through her purse to get her phone and sent Johnny a frantic text message: "CALL ME WHEN YOU GET A CHANCE!"

Forget dinner, there was no way she could eat now until she knew whether or not Fiona was going to stamp her with a scarlet A in the pages of her divorce document.

Does she even know my name?

The thought gave Jaylah a momentary reprieve. Johnny wasn't stupid. He wouldn't give his ex-wife Jaylah's name as ammunition; he had probably told her that he'd met *someone.* Some vague, ambiguous woman who had reminded him what love was supposed to look like.

Jaylah exhaled and drained the last of her champagne, immediately wanting another glass.

"Dammit," she said under her breath, knowing that another round of bubbly would be irresponsible, although it might calm the jumble of nerves growing in her gut.

She fired off another message. "Does Fiona know my name???? Is she naming me in the petition??? I NEED TO KNOW!"

Jaylah fidgeted in place like someone trying to conceal a drug habit. Normal movements like gazing around the room, or checking her phone, or waiting for Jourdan to drift back over and put her mind at ease suddenly looked manic and uneasy. She thought about leaving and running off to find Johnny again, but she couldn't do that to her girl. She promised Jourdan she'd be here, and no matter how uncomfortable or crazy she looked, she was staying until her friend was ready to leave.

Instead of grabbing another drink or heading to the exit Jaylah decided to walk around and actually look at the art. She hoped focusing on something other than the shitstorm brewing in her mind would release the knot growing in her belly.

After checking out a group of black and white photographs chronicling Brixton in the 1970s and 1980s,

Jaylah paused in front of a painting of a naked woman with wild hair and round hips. The woman was leaning against a multicolored wall, her expression lusty yet forlorn, and her hands gesturing to someone that was out of the frame. Jaylah couldn't take her eyes off the woman whose dewy brown skin made her seem regal and almost otherworldly.

"You like that one?" a man's voice said from behind her. Jaylah nodded, but never took her eyes off the canvas. "She reminds me of you."

Jaylah laughed to herself. *How could this magnificent woman remind anyone of me?* she wanted to ask, but she politely thanked the man without looking in his direction.

"I'm serious, Jaylah," he said, rolling her name through his mouth like it was a familiar tune. Jaylah's headed ricocheted toward the voice, and she saw the man shrug. "You were my muse."

She studied his face, took in his thick eyebrows, perfect olive skin, and gorgeous brown eyes. He smiled and a bolt of electricity shot through her body as a scene from their night together flashed through her head. "Faraj…"

He stepped in close, gently kissed both her cheeks and squeezed her hand. "It's been a while, yeah? I guess that night wasn't as great as I remember."

Jaylah blushed. He had it wrong, all wrong. Their night together was incredible. Jaylah had never had the gall to take a man she'd met in a club home, but there was something about Faraj she just had to have. He looked at her with unabashed desire and it made her feel sexy in a way that she'd never felt before that night. Jaylah could have easily gone back for more, *much more*, but she told herself that she didn't want to get caught up in anything serious.

She shook her head; that's exactly what she'd gone and done anyway.

"No...it was," she admitted quietly. Faraj was standing so close Jaylah could smell his scent, an intoxicating mixture of ylang ylang and sandalwood; she had to stop herself from inhaling. "I just...I wasn't planning on staying in London," she stammered. "I...I was only supposed to be here for a few months and I didn't want to get too involved and then leave."

"But now you're here..." Faraj said, letting the rest of his sentence trail off in a way that signaled he wanted whatever she was willing to give.

"Yeah..." Jaylah fidgeted like a crackhead again. "I am."

He broke their gaze and turned to the painting that had captured her attention in the first place.

"I painted this about a month after we met. You never called and I still couldn't get you out of my mind. This is the only thing I could think to do to get over you," he said meeting her eyes again. "But it didn't quite work, innit?"

Her face grew warm, and Jaylah felt a familiar tingling building between her thighs. For the first time since they met, Johnny wasn't the only man turning her on.

"So what made you stay in London? A man?" Faraj asked, his eyes hoping for a different answer than the one he offered.

Jaylah cleared her throat, trying to quell the desire creeping its way through her body. "I got a job," she spluttered. "With *Glamour*. I write a column."

"Oh really? About sex and love? Girly things?" he said, chuckling.

She found her voice. If there was one thing Jaylah could talk about without feeling awkward no matter who she was speaking to it was work. "No. I cover lots of different things—theater, restaurants, music, art. Basically if it's hot in London I want to write about it."

"Am I hot enough to be in your column?" he said, dropping his voice a seductive whisper.

Jaylah resisted the urge to bit her lip. Faraj was hot enough to be anywhere he damn-well pleased. A memory of them making out in the back of a cab flashed before her eyes but she quickly tried to push it out of her her brain. "Well, it looks like you might be. For starters you're in this show."

"So, how can I convince you to write about me? Do I need to take you to dinner?" He smirked.

"I'd need to see more of your work, hear your back-story. You know the usual," Jaylah said, trying to keep things strictly business.

"Okay, come by my studio tomorrow. It's in Clapham. I'll show you everything I have."

"Tomorrow probably won't work—"

"Then come tonight."

"Not happening," she said, enjoying their playful tête-à-tête.

Faraj laughed and threw up his hands. "I had to give it a shot. How about this. You give me a call when you're ready for me and we'll hook up."

When you're ready for me...

Faraj's double entendre echoed through her head, but Jaylah ignored it, excited by the idea of breaking a relatively new artist in her column. "Okay. I just need your number again, do you have some paper?"

He grabbed her phone, which she was still clutching in her hand, and punched in his number. Then Faraj stepped in close and whispered in her ear. "Now you won't lose it. I'm available," he said, kissing Jaylah on the cheek again, "whenever you want me."

Calling Faraj was as risky as lighting a match in a drought-ridden savannah, but as she watched him saunter away, Jaylah already knew that she would.

17

"I need you to talk me out of something," Jaylah said, as she walked to the Tube on her way to Faraj's studio in Clapham. It had been a week since they'd bumped into each other at the 30 Under 30 exhibit and for the last seven days Jaylah had been trying to talk herself out of seeing him again. But when she pitched the idea to her editor, Hillary seemed excited about featuring one of London's budding artists before he blew up.

"You could be like Philip Faflick," Hillary had said when Jaylah mentioned Faraj.

"Philip who?"

"The first reporter to write about Basquiat," she said like it was common knowledge.

"I doubt Faraj is the next Basquiat, Hillary." The thought sounded completely ridiculous. Based on his paintings at the exhibit it was clear Faraj was talented, but the next SAMO? Jaylah couldn't fathom it.

"Basquiat wasn't Basquiat back when Faflick wrote about him. He was just some homeless kid from Brooklyn. This could be big for us, Jaylah, especially if he turns out to be really talented."

Jaylah knew Hillary had a point, but the thought of being close to Faraj frightened her. Not because he was dangerous, or she thought he would hurt her, but because she was so excited to be near him again.

"What exactly am I talking you out of?" Jourdan asked, bringing Jaylah back to the present.

"I'm meeting Faraj in an hour to see his work."

"Faraj from the show? Wonderful! But why do you want me to talk you out of it?"

"Because...it's Faraj. And I shouldn't see him, right?" Jaylah sighed, hoping her friend would convince her to skip the appointment. She had reached the train station and was pacing back and forth, weighing her options.

"I don't understand. Why shouldn't you see him?"

"You don't remember Faraj?" Jaylah asked.

"Yes, of course. He was one of the artists from the 30 Under 30 show, yeah?"

"Well, yes, but—" Jaylah exhaled, it was clear Jourdan had forgotten all about the man Jaylah danced with the night the women first hung out. It was seven months ago and Jourdan had left them alone to get acquainted and make out with another man across the room. Perhaps she really didn't remember him.

Jaylah stood at the entrance of Arsenal Station trying to decide if she should head down the tunnel and get on the train or if she should go back to her flat. Of course she didn't reveal her tentativeness about meeting Faraj to Johnny. She only mentioned their interview, but left the details of their meeting—and their history—completely out of the conversation. *Why complicate things?* she told herself, especially when this was only work.

Still, Jaylah was uncertain she should see Faraj at all and hoped Jourdan would give her a reason to call the whole thing off.

"Ali Baba," Jaylah finally said, hoping Jourdan's off-the-cuff nickname for Faraj would jog her memory of that night. "He's is Ali Baba, remember?"

"Shut up!" Jourdan squealed into the phone. "No fucking way!"

"Yeah." Jaylah rubbed her temples, thankful she and Jourdan were finally on the same page. "Now you see why I shouldn't go?"

"Not really. That was like a million years ago."

"Seven months," Jaylah corrected her.

"Same thing. Look, I'm sure he's forgotten all about it by now."

Jaylah lowered her voice when she saw the man at the newsstand smiling at her. He'd seen her and Johnny together on several occasions and always commented that he was a lucky man to have such a beautiful girlfriend. Jaylah didn't need him overhearing her conversation and passing it along to Johnny when he bought the *Financial Times* on his way to the office.

"His painting in the show was about me. He said I was his muse," she said in a hushed tone. "And not for nothing, but he didn't *sound* like he was over it when we spoke at the gallery."

"Didn't he notice you're engaged? I can spot that ring from a mile away."

Jaylah peeked at the newspaper man again. "I wasn't wearing it."

"Are you wearing now?" Jourdan quizzed, and Jaylah glanced at her empty finger as if she'd forgotten the ring was still in the box on top of her dresser. She shook her head even though Jourdan couldn't see her.

"You need to tell him," Jourdan said, probably sensing Jaylah's silence meant she wasn't wearing the ring. "And you need to tell Johnny that you're have doubts about getting married."

Jaylah suddenly felt like she had been slapped. Her voice rose higher than she intended.

"I don't have doubts," she objected to Jourdan's accusation, even though it was true. She did have doubts, about *everything*. If she'd be a good mother, if she and Johnny would survive his drama, if she was ready to have her life altered in the most jarring of ways—twice.

"What would you call it then? Because that man thinks you're engaged and you're running around without your ring."

"I...I...just," Jaylah stuttered, feeling uncomfortable at the thought of second-guessing her relationship with Johnny. "I just need more time. Everything's moving so fast. We just need to slow down a little, that's all."

"Then you need to tell him that, Jay. Listen, I know you love him, and I know he loves you, but you can't keep leading him on."

"I'm not leading him on!"

"Oh yeah? Then when's the wedding? Because I need to buy a new dress."

Jaylah fell silent. What could she say? Everything about her relationship with Johnny felt unsettled. She wouldn't even dream of setting a wedding date until his divorce was final, and even then, she wasn't sure she was ready to be a mother *and* a wife all at once.

Just like that.

Her life had gone from completely unexciting to damn-near too much to bear in less than a year; the speed of the shift was utterly terrifying.

"Look, I need to pop out to meet with a client. But go see Faraj. Keep it professional, and if he tries anything, call me. I'll straighten him out."

Jaylah chucked at her friend's overprotectiveness. Between her mother, Johnny, and Jourdan, Jaylah had a crew of people who had her back and would run her life if she let them. She was thankful for all of them, but sometimes, especially with Johnny and her mother, their level of concern felt suffocating.

"Jaylah," Jourdan said, softening her tone. "You need to talk to Johnny. He deserves to know how you feel and you deserve to be heard."

"I know," Jaylah whispered. Jourdan was right. She had to talk to Johnny, especially if she wanted them to make it as a couple. Jaylah couldn't let her doubts fester and turn into an incurable cancer that would drag them both down. Even though she wanted to slow things down, she couldn't comprehend not having him in her life.

"I love you, sissy."

"I know," Jaylah said, turning to head into the station. Before descending the stairs into the tunnel, she paused, "Love you back."

◈◈◈◈◈

As soon as he opened the door wearing a paint-speckled tank top and low-slung jeans, Jaylah knew she was in trouble. Faraj's smile was wide and welcoming, and his eyes shone like freshly polished mahogany. She followed him up the stairs to his crowded studio that also doubled as his flat, taking note of what looked like dozens of canvases leaning against the walls, which were already bursting with kaleidoscopisc paintings in every hue imaginable. Faraj's space was almost too much for her heightened senses to take, her attention stolen by one thing then distracted by another.

"Can I get you something to drink? I have beer, wine, water?" he asked, standing next to her as she spun in a slow circle taking it all in.

"Water. The colder the better, please."

He disappeared into the kitchen and Jaylah walked around the airy living room, which appeared larger because of the row of bay windows facing Kings Avenue. She moved through his flat inspecting exotic-looking knickknacks and trinkets from his travels, then Jaylah paused at the mantle, gazing at a photo of Faraj riding a camel in the middle of the desert. Even though a scarf covered his face and head, she knew, just by looking at the intensity of the person's eyes, it was Faraj.

"How old were you here?" she asked when he returned with her water.

"Twenty."

"Why were you so sad?"

He stepped next to her and their arms touched; a pang of electricity shot through her frame. "What makes you think I was sad?"

She shrugged. "I can just tell. Your eyes kinda give you away, and I don't sense a smile."

Faraj was silent for a moment, then moved closer to the picture, inspecting it like he needed to get a closer look. "I had just buried my father the day before this was taken. I was feeling lost, like I was a ship without an anchor." He picked up another photo of a smiling woman who had Faraj's dark, sparkling eyes. "My mother," he said, showing Jaylah the picture, "she died when I was 16. So when my dad died, I just felt completely alone."

"Oh Faraj, I'm sorry—"

He waved off her condolences, stopping her midsentence. "It's not your fault." Faraj put the picture of his mother back on the ledge and seemed to get lost in his memories. Although it would probably make for a juicy backstory—struggling orphaned artist makes good—Jaylah suddenly felt like she was intruding.

"I think we should change the subject." She tried to smile even though he wasn't looking in her direction. "Let's talk about something else, yeah?"

"My father was an artist," Faraj said, ignoring Jaylah's proposed subject change. "He moved here from Morocco back in the 70s to study engineering at Imperial College. He was a very successful petroleum engineer, but in here," Faraj pounded his chest, "he was an artist."

Jaylah felt like she should be taking notes or recoding Faraj's history for the article, but she didn't want to cheapen the moment. Instead, she just listened, transcribing all of the details to her memory.

"My mother was like the sun—bright, brilliant, sometimes blinding. She was all heart, all passion. She reminded my father of his art, even when he was forced to pursue other things to make money. She was the living, breathing embodiment of his work. My mother was his muse. And when she died..." his voice trailed off and he was silent again.

As a seasoned interviewer Jaylah knew she couldn't rush him. Moreover, she wouldn't step on his recollections, because in truth, the silence made her feel closer to him. Although they had slept together Jaylah didn't know anything about Faraj, or where he came from. Like the stories of the people who allowed her into their space, it drew her in.

So she waited, what else could she do?

After gazing at the photographs for several minutes Faraj opened up once again. "When my mother died, the fire seemed to go out in my father's eyes. His passion was snuffed out, and soon, he was a zombie— walking around, but not living, innit. I knew it was only a matter of time before he joined her."

Faraj picked up the picture of him trekking through the desert and grimaced. "You were right, Jaylah, I was incredibly sad. After my mother passed away, my father said he wanted to be buried next to her back home, so I made sure to carry out his wishes. But when the ceremony was over I felt restless, like I needed to do something but didn't know what." He turned to look at her then. "Have you ever felt like that?"

"Yes," she said slightly above a whisper. "That's how I ended up in London."

"Then you understand," he said. "I was born here, you know. I only remember going to Morocco a handful of times. But for some reason I had this overwhelming need to reconnect to the land, to the people, *my people*. I hired a guide and I rode across the Sahara from Fez to Marrakech, just winding my way across the Merzouga Desert."

"Wow, that must have been incredible."

"It was." Faraj smiled for the first time since Jaylah inquired about the picture; she felt relieved. "I watched the sun rise over the sand dunes, and even though they were gone, I felt so connected to my parents. It turned out to be one of the best experiences of my life. That's when I decided to pursue my art. My father wished he could have, but he felt obligated to my mother and me. But I didn't have anyone to be responsible for, so I just went for it. That's sort of how I live my life. I just go for it."

"And do you usually get what you want?"

"Not always," he said looking into her eyes, "but it never stops me from trying."

Faraj let his words dance in the air, and Jaylah focused all of her energy on keeping her feelings in check. The last thing she needed was to *feel* something for this man who seemed so willing to let her in to his most private moments, but she couldn't help it. Something about Faraj's openness made her want to know more.

He smiled again, splintering some of the tension between them. "Sorry, I'm supposed to be showing you
my work, not telling you my sob story."

"No, no. This is great," she said, trying to sound
aloof and professional. "It helps me get inside your
head and see what makes you tick."

He smirked. "I don't know if you want to see what's
inside my head."

"Of course I do. It'll help me write a more in depth
profile."

Jaylah was full of shit and she knew it. She stole a
glance at his lips and wondered if they were still as soft
as the night they kissed. For the last week, flashes of
their passionate evening flickered through her memory,
and no matter how hard she tried to forget, Jaylah just
couldn't shake how good his tongue felt all over her
skin. She cleared her throat hoping to mask her desire.
"People love a good backstory and it sounds like you
have a very interesting one. I'm excited about this."

"Oh. Me too," he said, grinning like a sneaky child.
"You look really beautiful, by the way. I meant to tell
you that when you got here."

Jaylah nervously ran her hand over the mop of curls
that had multiplied in size since she got off the train
and walked the half-mile to Faraj's flat. The damp afternoon had turned her somewhat tame twist-out into
a wild, wavy 'fro that rivaled Chaka Khan's. Jaylah
wished she'd brought a hair tie to pull it back so she
could still look presentable. After ripping through her

closet to find something to wear, she decided on a pair of black jeans and an indigo peplum top that hid the beginnings of her baby bump. Jaylah thought she looked good, but not *beautiful.*

"Thank you," she said, blushing as she watched Faraj's eyes sweep over her again. "So...umm...can I see some of your stuff? It looks like you're drowning in canvases."

"Sure, I'll show you what I'm working on now."

Faraj led Jaylah into another room that had about a half-dozen sketches taped to the walls and a blank canvas perched on an easel. The sketches were of women in various poses—sitting, standing, dancing—and in various states of undress. They were all rough and unfinished, but still impressive.

"Are these a part of a portrait series?"

"Yeah. I'm trying to decide if I want to paint several women or just one woman. But I haven't really been inspired by any of them."

"What's this?" Jaylah asked, uncovering a group of paintings that featured a woman similar to the one she'd seen in the gallery.

"Those are from an unfinished collection," he said closing the distance between them.

She cycled through the paintings and was in awe of the woman again. "But these look done. And they're lovely, Faraj." Jaylah held up a portrait of a brown skin woman in a body-hugging dress, pouty red lips, and a crush of untamed hair. She looked like she was dancing. "This one is...wow. It's dope."

"Of course it is. It's you," Faraj said, standing so close they were almost touching.

"This...she..." Jaylah stammered. "She can't be me. She looks..."

"Trust me. I painted her, remember?" He cocked a sly eyebrow.

Jaylah felt like she'd stepped into a sauna. Her body was warm and a familiar ache started building in her loins. She had to get out of there—quick—before she lost her head.

Jaylah put the painting down and moved to the other side of the room, hoping to put some distance between them. She needed a distraction from the lust edging up her body, but Faraj followed her, once again narrowing the space between them and setting her aflame.

"Pose for me," he said in a seductive hush.

"What? Don't be silly, Faraj. I'm not a model."

"So what. I painted those others after I saw you at the gallery. It was crazy. It was like I was possessed. I didn't stop for like four days, I was so inspired. Pose for me, please?"

"I...I...don't think that will be a good idea," she sputtered, suddenly ready to leave Faraj's flat. "I'm supposed to be objective remember? I'm writing a story about you, I can't be *in* the story."

"Just think about it. It would mean the world to me, Jaylah. Please just consider it."

Damn, he's even sexier when he begs. Get out of here girl. NOW.

"I'll think about it, Faraj, but..." she looked at her watch like it mattered what time it was. "I have to get going. I have another appointment and it's all the way in Shoreditch."

"Let me give you a lift."

"You don't have to do that, I'm just going to jump on the Tube and..."

"It's no problem, really," he said cutting her off. "I have to deliver a painting to Clerkenwell and another to Marylebone. One of the pieces from he opening sold."

"Which one? The woman?"

"No, that one isn't for sale. I'm keeping that one...for my private collection," he said, moving a wayward piece of hair out of her face.

Jaylah turned her back, trying to will her emotions under control. This afternoon with Faraj was supposed to be strictly business; she was there to interview him, see his artwork, and leave. But instead Jaylah was blushing like a schoolgirl who finally caught the attention of the cutest boy in school.

"So, which ones did you sell?" she asked, hoping the change in subject would stop their flirting.

He crossed the room and pulled a drop cloth off of a gigantic canvas depicting a couple strolling down the glittery streets of the West End.

"This one was commissioned. This older gentlemen had me paint it for his wife. He took her to the theater on their first date 30 years ago and someone snapped their picture, but they lost it in a fire."

"She's going to *love* this. We women go crazy over shit like this."

"Why? Because it's romantic?" he chuckled.

"No, it shows that he cares, and he was obviously paying attention. That's what women really want, you know. To be seen."

"Even you?" he asked, walking back over to her.

Yes," Jaylah admitted quietly. "Even me."

"Good, because I can't keep my eyes off of you."

Faraj stood directly in front of Jaylah and tilted her chin up. He paused to stare into her eyes and appeared to study her face before he leaned in to kiss her.

Jaylah knew it was wrong. How could she just stand there and let another man cover her mouth with his? But she couldn't move. It was as if her feet were nailed to the floor, preventing her from running away.

Faraj traced her nose, then the outline of her lips before gently taking her head in his hands and bringing it closer to him.

She waited to feel his warmth and taste his tongue as it slipped into her mouth, but just before their lips met her phone blared, shocking her back to her senses.

She fumbled through her bag to silence the ringer, but she noticed it was Johnny.

Jaylah held up a finger and then turned her back on Faraj. "Hello?"

"Hey," he said, sounding excited. "I have some news. Can you meet me at my office?"

"Everything okay?"

"It might be," he said, and Jaylah's heart beat faster. Between almost kissing Faraj and whatever Johnny had to tell her, she wasn't sure she could take any more excitement for the day. "Babes, I'll explain when I see you. Can you get here in a hour?"

"Yeah...that should work," she said turning to look at Faraj who was waiting patiently while she wrapped up her conversation.

"Good," Johnny sighed, "I love you."

"You too."

Jaylah hung up the phone and thanked God for saving her from a major fuckup. She couldn't believe how close she came to kissing Faraj and possibly cheating on the man she loved.

What the hell were you thinking, Jay? she asked herself while she eyed Faraj—sexy, vulnerable, passionate Faraj.

Okay. You've really got to get out of here!

"Faraj, I gotta get going," she said, already moving toward the stairs. "I appreciate the offer to drop me off, but I really don't want to bother you and I'm cool.

I'll call you later to set up a time for us to talk again for the profile. I think it's going to be great!"

"Jaylah...should we talk about this?"

She shooed away the mention of their almost kiss. "No need. We both got a little caught up," she said. "Won't happen again."

Jaylah regretted adding that last bit when she saw his shoulders deflate and a sad look flood his eyes. She didn't want to hurt Faraj's feelings; as a matter of fact, she *really* wanted to kiss him. But that just wasn't the best idea. Not when she was in love with Johnny and pregnant with his child.

No, no mater how gorgeous and mysterious and exciting Faraj was, he needed to remain part of her history, not her future. She couldn't let him complicate her life; she had enough of that already.

And now Johnny had news.

Jaylah just hoped it was something good.

18

Jaylah waited for the elevator on the ground floor of One Canada Square, a posh skyscraper in Canary Wharf that housed many of the city's financial intuitions. She paced the aisle during the entire 40-minute train ride to Johnny's office wondering what was so important he had to share it in person.

Johnny rarely let his emotions get the better of him. While every shift in Jaylah's mood flashed across her face, he kept his feelings in check, choosing to project an unshakable air of confidence, even when things were falling apart. So when he called to tell Jaylah he had some news, she knew it had to be big.

"Hello, I'm here to see Mr. Poku," she told the receptionist when she got off the elevator on the 27th floor. The offices of JPFS, Inc.—a mash-up of Johnny's initials and that of his partner Femi Solade—were modern and beige, standard fare for the stuffy firms housed in Canary Wharf.

"Your name, miss?"

"Jaylah Baldwin," she said, suddenly aware that this was the first time she'd been inside Johnny's office. Whenever they'd meet after work or for lunch he'd be downstairs in the lobby waiting for her. It struck Jaylah as both odd and amusing that he'd finally invited her up.

"Oh yes, he's expecting you," the woman said with a wide smile. "Take a right and Mr. Poku's office is at the end of the corridor."

"Thank you."

"And congratulations!" the woman called behind Jaylah as she headed down the hallway.

When she got to Johnny's door, Jaylah paused and said a little prayer that she could handle whatever he was about to say. She told herself that she would not, under any circumstances, make a scene that would embarrass either one of them, and she was absolutely not going to cry—pregnancy hormones be dammed.

Jaylah knocked on the door and waited for Johnny's voice to welcome her in, but instead he flung it open and hugged her like he hadn't seen her in weeks. Then he kissed her. Not a polite, run-of-the-mill kiss, but a passionate I-want-to-tear-your-clothes-off lip-lock.

"I'm glad you could make it, babes," he said, face stretched into a big grin. He turned and introduced her to a man sitting in the corner of the room. "Jaylah this is Charles Barrington."

"Oh...hello," she said, slightly embarrassed and caught off guard that Johnny would kiss her so passionately when someone else was in the room.

The man stood and extended his hand. "Nice to meet you, Jaylah. I've heard so much about you." She looked at Johnny who was still smiling, wondering what had been said.

Who was this man? And why has he heard so much about me?

"I can wait in the lobby. I didn't mean to interrupt your meeting," she stammered, feeling off balance by the entire scene.

"No, Charles is my barrister. He's why I called."

"Oh? I don't understand...what's the news?"

"It's about Fiona." Jaylah's body tensed at the mention of his ex-wife's name. Even though Johnny seemed happy about whatever was going on, Jaylah braced herself just in case a bomb was about to go off. "Charles will explain everything. Charles?"

Johnny led Jaylah to the seat next to his lawyer.

"We believe Ms. O'leary is going to accepting our settlement offer. We've been going back and forth all week with her solicitor, but he said they'll give us an answer this afternoon."

Charles smiled at Jaylah and she felt like she should speak up. "Oh great." Jaylah tried to sound excited, but she was still worried. "But...how can you be sure she'll accept the offer? Last week she decided to file her own petition, what's changed?"

"Like I told Jonathan, that was merely a negotiation tactic. She never actually filed the petition. She just wanted more money."

"And you've given it to her?" Jaylah asked.

"We increased our offer. It's more than generous. Her other demands were a little unreasonable."

Jaylah was curious about Fiona's other requests. Did they include her? Was she pissed about the baby? Did she even know?

"Like what?"

Charles looked at Johnny as if to ask for permission to discuss his divorce proceedings with Jaylah. Johnny nodded and Charles continued talking.

"Well, she wanted to keep the house, her car, and half of his assets, which amounted to about five million pounds."

"Five million pounds...." Jaylah repeated like she wasn't sure if she'd heard Charles correctly. She knew Johnny wasn't struggling, but Jaylah didn't realize he was a millionaire. Aside from his shiny Mercedes and well-tailored suits, Johnny wasn't flashy. He didn't waste money on frivolous things like expensive gadgets or gaudy jewelry, and his uniform was always the same: suit, dress shoes, and an understated watch when he was working; a pair of jeans and a button-down shirt when he was not. Moreover, nothing about his demeanor screamed wealthy—he wasn't entitled, he worked his ass off, and he never talked down to anyone. So when Jaylah heard that half of his assets amounted to more than she'd probably earn in a lifetime she was thrown for a loop.

"Exactly. Completely unreasonable," Charles said, "especially since Jonathan founded this firm before they were married and had already made several of the deals that would net him millions. She had no claims to it really. Her petition was like a Hail Mary pass."

Jaylah's head was still swimming. *A millionaire? Johnny is a millionaire?*

"And now you think she'll accept the settlement?"

"Definitely. We told them two-and-a-half million was our best offer, and if she wanted more they'd have to see us in court."

"What happens if she decides to go to court? Will I be dragged into this? I'm here on a VISA, you know, I can't afford for anything to mess that up."

Johnny spoke up then, caressing her hand. "I wouldn't let that happen, Jay." His eyes were resolute and assured, a familiar look. "You know that."

The first time she'd seen this look was way back in the beginning. They were getting ready to leave the Jazz Café when a man approached Jaylah and asked for a dance. When she declined he pressed the issue, grabbing her arm and whispering something lewd in her ear. Before she could react, Johnny stepped between them, daring the man to put his hands on her again *or else*. The man got loud, threating to mash Johnny up, but he never wavered, he just glared at the man like he would go off if he did more than talk. The man finally slunk away, and Jaylah was impressed that Johnny had not only stepped in to protect her, but also refused to back down when the man became increasingly belligerent.

Jaylah knew Johnny would do everything in his power to protect her, but if Fiona decided to take their battle to court, she couldn't be sure that he could.

"*If* they go to court," Charles spoke again, "she'll need a new solicitor. I'll eat that guy alive," he chuckled. Jaylah could see why Johnny hired Charles, they both operated on the same inordinate amount of self-assurance that seemed almost foreign to most others.

Charles' phone rang and he looked at Johnny. It was Fiona's attorney calling with an answer. As they listened to pieces of the one-sided conversation, Johnny stroked her hand while they stared at Charles intently, trying to decipher Fiona's answer from his responses.

"I see. Yes, well, you know that's our final offer and we feel like it's more than generous." Charles was up on his feet, pacing the room as he talked. "I understand, but if we go before the judge we'll argue for less. And you know my track record, Hugh." Jaylah watched the portly man, her heart beating wildly at the idea that they were close to end of Johnny's divorce.

Jaylah had prayed the proceedings would be over by the time she had the baby in June, but now that it could possibly be settled in a matter of weeks, she was once again confronted with her uncertainty about getting married. No matter what happened, she and Johnny needed to talk about it soon.

"Well," Charles said when he got off the phone, "they've agreed to our terms. I'll file the decree nisi tomorrow, and in six weeks, if everything goes according to plan, you'll officially be divorced."

"Brilliant! That's just brilliant," Johnny said, shaking his lawyer's hand. "Thanks for all of your hard work, Charles. It really means a lot to me." He turned to hug Jaylah. "To us. It means the world to us, man. Thank you."

"My pleasure. I'll leave you two alone to celebrate," he said, winking at Jaylah. "Jonathan, I'll have my secretary send over a copy of the papers on Monday."

Johnny led Charles out of his office and rushed back over to Jaylah. "My God, I'm so happy," he said, picking her up and spinning her around. "No more purgatory! Now we can move on with our lives, innit."

His energy was infectious and Jaylah couldn't help but be caught up in his jubilation. A weight *had* been lifted from their backs. Johnny wouldn't be married to another woman when their was child born, and perhaps, with the divorce proceedings coming to an end, Jaylah could finally let go of her guilt and get on with their lives.

But there was just one more hurdle they needed to clear: her apprehension about getting married.

"Congrats, Mr. Poku," Jaylah said, wrapping her arms around his neck and placing a kiss on his chin. "There's just one problem…"

He pulled back to look at her, concern etching his face. "What's that?"

"So….you're a millionaire?"

He broke out in a throaty laugh. "And that's a problem?"

"How come you didn't tell me?"

"How was I supposed to tell you? Hello, I'm Johnny, I'm a millionaire?" he chuckled some more. "It's not something I talk about anyway. It's just money, it's not that important."

"So what else have you been hiding from me?" Jaylah said, keeping her tone playful.

He kissed her neck, then parted her lips with his tongue. "Nothing. There's nothing else."

"Are you sure?" she quizzed.

"Umm hmm. As a matter of fact," he paused to kiss her again, "I wanted to set up a meeting with my accountant so we could go over everything. I need to update my insurance polices to make certain you and the baby are taken care of in case…"

She put a finger to his mouth, hushing him. "I don't want to think about that."

"I know, but we have to plan for the worst and hope for the best, babes."

The worst. Jaylah didn't even want to entertain the possibility of Johnny dying and leaving her alone with a baby—even if she had enough money to tide her over for a lifetime. She wanted him.

"Charles thinks we should get a pre-nup."

Jaylah bristled. *The worst. He's already planning for our demise.*

"And what do you think?"

"I think he's a jaded bloke who handles too many divorces," Johnny chortled. "I told him to forget about it."

"I would think someone in your position would consider it. Didn't you just say 'hope for the best, plan for the worst?'"

Johnny pulled her away from his chest again and looked her in the eyes. "Yeah, but I'm in this forever, Jaylah."

"You promised Fiona the same thing..."

"I did, but I didn't mean it," he admitted. "I didn't even want to get married. It just seemed like the responsible thing to do."

"And now..." Jaylah touched her stomach, "are you just being responsible?"

"Yes, of course," he said covering her hand with his, "but I'm also crazy about you. Like, completely mad."

Jaylah searched his eyes for answers, and he didn't flinch or waver under her gaze. He allowed her to study his face, probably hoping whatever she saw put her fears at ease.

"And if I wasn't pregnant, would you still..."

"Of course, I would," he said, cutting her off. "I'm not here because of the baby, Jaylah. I didn't turn my life inside out just because of our child. Don't get me wrong, I'm over the fucking moon about being a father, but I did this for you. For us. I love you. I loved you before I even knew you were pregnant, remember? And I love you now. This isn't a fad, Jay. I'm not going to stop loving you tomorrow or the next day or the next."

"And years from now? When things aren't so new and exciting? What about then?"

"I'll still love you."

"You promise?" she asked, tears gathering in her eyes.

Johnny drew an imaginary X over his chest. "Forever, forever, ever."

Jaylah prayed she could say the same.

19

Johnny's alarm went off at seven a.m. and Jaylah instinctively rolled over and sat on the edge of the bed. Although she worked from home, Jaylah didn't want to fall into the seductive trap of lazing around the house for house before researching, writing, or brainstorming for her column. Because of this, when Johnny rose each morning to begin getting ready for work, she did as well.

"Come back to bed," he mumbled. Still half-asleep, Johnny switched off the alarm and rolled over, pulling her back into his arms.

"You're not feeling well?" she asked, confused that he wasn't already in the bathroom turning on the shower. Johnny was meticulous about being on time. Every morning he was out the door by 7:45 so he could catch the 8:07 train and get to the office before nine.

In the months they'd been cohabiting he'd *never* slept in during the week, even on bank holidays. "*The rest of the world is at work, Jaylah, so I need to be too,*" he'd said the last time she thought he'd skip his alarm and stay in bed.

But today was different. Johnny wrapped his arms around Jaylah and nuzzled her neck.

"I feel wonderful."

She stretched out her hand and put it to his head to see if it was warm, just in case.

He chuckled. "I'm fine, Jaylah. Seriously."

"But you never sleep through the alarm, what's up?"

"Taking the day off."

"Taking the day off?" It must have been the sleepiness talking, she figured. "You've never taken the day off."

"I know. But between wrapping up that deal with the Barbedos Group, and Fiona agreeing to our terms, I think I deserve a long weekend, innit."

"Great!" She clapped, excited to have an extra pair of hands. "You can help me run a few errands. Let's see, I have to go to the dry cleaners, pick up a few things from Boots, run to the…"

"No errands." He kissed her neck. "Let's do something fun."

"Fun? On a workday?"

"I'm off today, remember? No work."

He moved a hand to her stomach, resting it there.

"Okay...let's go to see that movie that just came out, what's the name of it again..."

"No movies. Let's do something we wouldn't normally do. Like you said, I rarely take the day off, so let's make the most of it."

"What do you have in mind?" she asked, tracing his knuckles as his hand caressed her belly.

"Well..." he hummed into her neck. "We can go away for the weekend."

"Away? Where?"

"Ever been to Bordeaux?"

She turned to face him, eyes widening. "France?"

"Umm hmm," he sang, stroking the side of her face.

"I was supposed to go to Paris last year, but the trip fell through. I haven't been to France yet, but I've been dreaming about it since forever."

"Then we're definitely going."

Johnny kissed her nose, then got up and grabbed his MacBook. He flipped it open and began searching for flights to Bordeaux.

"We can't go to France just like that."

He gave her a quick glance and continued Googling flights. "Why not? Do you have to work this weekend?"

"No…" Jaylah ran her calendar through her head, and then checked her phone just to be sure. "I don't have to cover an event until Tuesday, but I was gonna to catch up on things around the house. My laundry is piling up, I haven't done it in forever."

"Forget the laundry. We're going away for the weekend."

She looked at him in disbelief. "To France?"

"Umm hmm."

While Johnny scrolled through flight options on the British Airways website, Jaylah went into the bathroom to wash her face. By the time she started brushing her teeth, Johnny had booked their tickets.

"We leave at 10, babes," he said, grabbing his toothbrush and getting to work on his pearly whites.

"Tonight?"

He spit out the mint paste. "No, this morning."

She looked at him like he'd lost his mind. "That's in less than three hours. There's no way we can pack and get to Heathrow by then. You know it's always a madhouse."

"We're leaving from Gatwick. It's only a half hour away, and we can certainlly make it if you just throw a few things in a bag."

"What if I forget something?"

Johnny grabbed her around the waist and smacked his lips against her cheek.

"We'll buy it there, babes. They have stores, you know."

Johnny turned on the shower, stripped off his clothes, and stepped inside. They were going to France. *Just like that.* Jaylah marveled at how quickly he'd made up his mind and bought the tickets. She and Johnny had always explored the city together, but their outings were usually confined to weekends, and big things—like going to the theater or taking in a concert—were always planned. Johnny was a lot of things, but spontaneous wasn't typically one of them.

I can get used to this, she thought.

Jaylah pulled her t-shirt over her head and tossed it in the hamper before joining Johnny in the shower. His eyes doubled in size when he saw her.

Johnny shook his head, a smirk inching across his lips.

"You're going to make us late."

She found his lips and pressed her breasts into his firm chest. "Not if you hurry up."

⟨❈⟩

Jaylah and Johnny strolled along the banks of the Garonne heading across the Pont de Pierre at dusk. They had taken the tram across the ancient stone bridge earlier in the afternoon, but as the sun streaked across the sky, retreating for the evening, she insisted they walk.

"Isn't this just…." Jaylah's voice trailed off, unable to articulate exactly what she was experiencing. The dark river lapped at the foot of the bridge's seventeen arches, one for each letter in Napoléon Bonaparte's name, and antique lamps illuminated their path. The entire scene made Jaylah feel like she'd been transposed into the lines of a Victor Hugo poem. *Romantic.* The tableau was simply romantic.

They had arrived in the city just before noon and checked into the Grand Hotel de Bordeaux, which reminded Jaylah of a palace with its ornate ceilings and luxurious décor. A bottle of Château Les Ormes de Pez greeted them as they entered the junior suite.

"Let's have a toast," she'd said, grabbing the bottle and searching for an opener.

Johnny cocked an eyebrow, but remained silent.

"What? We're on vacation, remember? Besides, pregnant women have wine all the..."

He took the bottle and kissed her on the lips. "I know, babes."

Johnny found the uncorker, popped the bottle, and then poured two glasses, before handing one to Jaylah. "Cheers."

"You know, I could seriously get used to New Johnny." She chuckled before taking a sip.

He grinned. "Me too."

They had spent the balance of the afternoon roaming around the Golden Triangle, seeing the old city, buying macaroons, and popping into the crowded boutiques along Rue Sainte-Catherine so Jaylah could look for earrings. Even though it was winter Bordeaux was bright and mesmerizing, and Jaylah loved every minute of its old world charm.

"Think we should head back to the hotel?" Johnny asked, wrapping his arms around Jaylah as the wind whooshed around the Pont de Pierre. She'd been gazing into the blackened river for several minutes, hypnotized by its ebb and flow. She hadn't even noticed the sudden rush of cold air.

"In a minute."

"Okay, I just don't want you to get sick. It's pretty nippy out here, yeah?"

She relaxed into his embrace and leaned her head against his chest. "I'm fine, Johnny."

"I know, babes." He snuggled her further as they watched a group of boats chugging across the water. "Sometimes..." he spoke quietly as if he was thinking out loud, "I wonder if you need me at all."

Jaylah turned to face him. Did she hear him correctly? Was he joking? Had this new, spontaneous creature caused her lover to lose his mind?

"What did you say?"

She eyed him trying to find a reason for his words, but she came up empty. Even though Jaylah thought herself as somewhat of a feminist, she had never thrown her independence in Johnny's face. She adored his chivalrous ways and would often wait while he opened doors for her and let him pick up the tab whenever they went out. But she refused to cave on the big stuff like quitting her job, or being a stay at home mom.

Truthfully, though, Jaylah didn't *need* Johnny in the practical sense of the word. She could take care of herself, and if their relationship went to shit, she would provide for the baby too. But even though she didn't *need* him to survive she wanted him. Badly.

"Where did that come from?"

"Sometimes..." he shrugged, "I just wonder."

Jaylah stared up at Johnny for a long while trying to organize her words. She stroked his face, hoping her tenderness would temper what she was about to say.

"I don't need your money, if that's what you mean. And yes, if you left me tomorrow I would be gutted. Like, completely and utterly devastated..."

"But..."

"I wouldn't die. Somehow, I would pick myself up and keep living. It would hurt, but I'd keep going."

He turned to peer at the river.

"I wouldn't," Johnny said just above a whisper.

"Yes, you would."

Jaylah laced her fingers through his and kissed the back of Johnny's hand.

"Just because I don't *need* you in that way doesn't mean I don't love you, and don't want you with every fiber of my being." She brought his face back to hers. "Because I do."

Johnny studied her eyes and she hoped he came up with the right answers.

"You remind me of my mum, you know. Beautiful, smart, and *very* spirited." He offered Jaylah a brief smile. "I just hope I'm not like my father."

"What do you mean?"

Johnny took in a deep breath through his nose and blew it out of his mouth slowly.

"My father...is a difficult man. Growing up my mum wanted to work. She went to uni to be a nurse, but when she married my father and had my older sister, he wanted her to stay home. And then my other sister and I were born, and my mum never had a chance to be a nurse."

"What about when you guys got older? She could have worked then, right?"

"You would think so, but my dad wouldn't allow it. He was completely inflexible and she gave up her dream. I kind of hated him for it."

"Those were just the times, Johnny. Back then, women stayed home while their husbands worked. Hell, my mother did the same thing. It was a different generation."

Johnny nodded, bobbing his head quickly.

"I understand that, but I know my mum wanted more. I asked her once, 'Mum what do you do all day when you're alone and we're at school?' Do you know what she said?"

He waited for an answer; Jaylah shook her head.

"Talk to the walls. Can you believe that?" he asked. "She was so bored and lonely she'd talk to the walls. I hated my father after that. I hated him because he wouldn't let her live her life, and because she loved him, like totally fucking loved him, she wouldn't even dare."

Johnny glanced at her and Jaylah's heart broke open at the site of his damp eyes. Before she could speak he continued talking.

"I don't want to be like him, Jaylah. He was so hard on me, you know. I'm his only son and nothing was ever good enough for him. When I got a B in university he'd ask why I hadn't gotten an A. When I started my firm he asked why I wanted to jeopardize my career on such a frivolous dream. I made a million pounds and he told me it could have been more had I stayed with HSBC. Nothing was ever good enough for him. *Nothing.*"

Johnny gripped the railing of the bridge and for a split second Jaylah thought he might just leap off, the look etched in his face seemed so full of pain. She circled her arms around his waist, pressed her head to his back, and listened.

"I bought him that house in Ghana, you know. I hired the architect, had it built, and gave it to my parents as a gift. And now I'm not welcome?" Johnny threw his hands in the air and his voice soared. "Everything I've done in my life I did to please him. Go to uni, study finance, marry Fiona—it's all been for *him.* And now that I've finally done something for me and he can't handle it and *I'm* the one cut out?" Johnny turned to Jaylah and caressed her face. "No, *he's* the one missing out, Jaylah. Him, not me. I have my own family now."

He hastily whipped his face with the back of his hand and tried to smile but it looked like a grimace instead.

"God, I sound mad, yeah? We're supposed to be having a good time. I'm sorry, babes. It's just...I don't want to be like him. I don't want you to feel like you have to give up your dreams for me."

"You're in luck because I wasn't planning to," she joked, trying to lighten his mood.

He chuckled for a moment before turning serious again. "I am proud of you, you know. The way you picked up and started a whole new life in London is nothing short of amazing. It takes guts. That's one of the things I love about you."

"My guts?" she said, patting her stomach still trying to get him to smile a real smile. "That's it?"

"Well, yes, and this." Johnny palmed her ass and they both giggled for several minutes. "But seriously, please let me know if I'm being overbearing. Don't walk around resenting me in silence, innit. I suffered with that for too long with my father, I wouldn't want you to hate me. I couldn't bear it."

"I could never hate you, Mr. Poku," she said, kissing him on the cheek.

He covered her mouth with his, parting her lips. "Good."

"But..." she said, causing him to pull back. "I think you should call your mom. Sounds like you miss her."

Johnny sighed. "I do."

"So call her. Maybe your dad will come around, maybe he won't. But I bet she wants to be a part of her grandchild's life."

"Yeah...she would." He turned toward the Garonne again. "She loves Bordeaux, you know. I sent my parents here for one of their anniversaries and she wouldn't stop talking about it. "

"Then it's settled. Promise you'll call her." She put her head on his chest and waited for an answer. "For me?"

"For you," he said, leaning down to kiss Jaylah's neck, "I'd do anything."

She slipped her hand in his and began gently pulling him down the walkway.

"Ditto."

20

"We should get married here," Johnny said as they walked along Rue Saint-Rémi after dinner. It was their last night in Bordeaux and they celebrated by dining at Le Gabriel, one of the finest restaurants in town. After seven decadent courses of fresh-baked bread with seaweed butter, roasted duck, Razor clams and diced sweet potatoes, assorted cheeses, and the most delectable chocolate soufflé she'd ever tasted, Jaylah suggested they amble through the streets on the way back to the hotel.

"Here in Bordeaux?"

Jaylah spoke before really giving either one of their questions a second thought; if she had, perhaps she would have held her tongue and let Johnny's statement dissipate into the cool evening. But all Jaylah knew was that she was in France, sauntering through the city on her lover's arm like a character in a Jean-Luc Godard film.

"Yeah, we could do it in the spring. The sun will be out, all the flowers will be in bloom, it'll be perfect, innit."

"And I'll be huge."

Jaylah couldn't imagine what she'd look like come April, two months shy of giving birth. She couldn't fathom being stuffed into a lacy white dress and waddling down the aisle to meet Johnny. Just the thought of it made her giggle.

She dismissed the idea. "I don't think so."

"But it would be très romantique," he said kissing the back of her hand as they moved past a group of tourists.

They turned onto Place de la Comédie and gazed at the Grand Théâtre, a magnificent structure whose stately columns glowed under the illuminated lamps. Jaylah marveled at the building, intoxicated by the mere sight of it. She spotted an oversized clock across from theater and decided to sit on its steps to soak it all in.

"This trip has been nothing short of amazing." She leaned over and kissed Johnny on the lips. "Thank you."

Jaylah threw her hands in the air. "Ohmygod, Johnny. Isn't it beautiful?"

He smiled at her. "Definitely, which is why I think it'll be perfect for the wedding."

Her mood shifted. *The wedding. Why the hell is he thinking about the wedding now?*

Their weekend in Bordeaux had confirmed what Jaylah already knew: she wanted to spend the rest of her life with Johnny.

Just when she thought she had him all figured out—hardworking, reliable, extremely protective—he surprised her with his sudden burst of spontaneity. And though he usually kept his inner-fears close to the vest, he'd allowed himself to open up and be vulnerable in a way that enlarged her heart.

But despite this, despite their absolutely perfect jaunt to France, Jaylah still did not want to rush off and get married as soon as Johnny's divorce was final. She wanted to be certain they weren't moving too quickly or skipping over the steps that would ensure a happily ever after.

Jaylah didn't want to tell him about needing to postpone the wedding; she feared Johnny wouldn't understand why she craved more time. But in spite of the risks, he had to know before her feelings turned into an ulcer that would kill them both.

"It would be pretty awesome to get married in France—"

"Right?" he said cutting in. "It would be so perfect."

"..But I think we should wait until after the baby's born. I mean..."

Johnny chuckled. "Please don't tell me you're self-conscious about showing. I know you'll be a stunning bride, even when you're seven months along."

She squeezed his hand. "Thanks, babe, but..."

"But what?"

Jaylah took a deep breath and told herself to say the words that had been sitting on the tip of her tongue for weeks.

"I want to wait until after the baby's born to get married. Way after."

He eyed her, and she averted his gaze. "I don't understand. Why?"

"What's the rush? With everything going on, why do we have to get married now?"

"The baby will be here in a few months, Jaylah."

"And? Why do we have to get married before it's born?"

"Because we're going to be a family..."

"We don't need a piece of paper to tell us that," she cut in.

"I know. But," he hesitated, blowing a quick burst of air through his lips, "I want to do this the right way, innit."

Jaylah sighed. She knew their sprint toward marriage was as much about honor as it was love. If nothing else, Johnny was an honorable man who wanted to do right by her and the baby. The trouble was, he didn't seem to realize he already had.

"Baby, nothing about our relationship has been done *the right way,*" she said. "We met when you were already married, for God's sakes. But this isn't the '50s, Johnny. No one is going to call our child a bastard or look at us sideways for not being married when it's born. And if they do, fuck them."

She stroked his hand and softened her tone.

"Can you honestly say, with everything that's going on, that you're ready to get married right now?"

Johnny straightened his back and met her gaze. "Yes."

Jaylah wanted to ask how he could be so sure. She wanted to know how he could have one marriage die, and be in the middle of burying it, and still be certain they would survive.

But she held her tongue.

"I guess you can't say the same?" he asked. "You don't want to marry me, Jaylah?"

Her chest constricted and Jaylah felt her heart splinter into a thousand jagged pieces when she saw the look on his face. Pain. Johnny's face was streaked with pain. Her words had sliced into him, opening a deep wound she wanted desperately to heal.

"Of course I want to marry you, Johnny. Of course."

"Then I don't understand. Why do you want to wait until after the baby's born?"

She took a deep breath. Johnny had said he loved her guts and her ability to take a chance. The time had come to finally spill it, and perhaps, put their relationship on the line for the truth.

"I just need more time."

"Because you're not sure about us?"

"Because I feel like everything's moving so fast I can barely keep up. Do you realize that a year ago I was back in L.A. writing for the *Weekly* and trying to figure out what the fuck I was going to do with my life?" She paused to take a breath. "And now," Jaylah shook her head like she didn't believe the story herself, "now I live in an entirely different country, finally have a job I enjoy, am four months pregnant with my first child, and am madly in love with a soon-to-be-divorced man who wants to get married *right now*. Baby, this shit is scary. Can't you understand that?"

"Of course I understand it. I'm scared too, Jay."

"So why are you in such a rush?"

He reached out to brush her hair behind her ear. "Because I love you, and—"

"You know how many people love each other and get divorced, Johnny? A coupe of years from now I don't want to be sitting across the room from you in court."

He grimaced.

"I just want you to know I'm not going anywhere, Jaylah. That I'm committed to you, to our family."

"Johnny I don't need a wedding to tell me what I already know, babe."

They sat in silence, watching people stroll by and Jaylah wondered why Johnny seemed to desperately need a piece of paper to feel secure. Didn't he know she was his from the moment they met? Didn't he realize she had forsaken all others after he'd pressed close to her that afternoon on the London Eye and watched the city open up beneath them?

Didn't he know she was already his?

The irony of the situation was not lost on Jaylah. Usually it was the woman who needed reassurance, an official commitment, and God's blessing. But this time, it was Johnny—confident, cocky, unshakable Johnny— who needed the guarantee.

"I'm not going anywhere, babe," she said, letting her thoughts spill over into words. "I've never felt this way about anyone. *Ever.* And I'm not giving it up."

Johnny put his arm around Jaylah's shoulder and she leaned into him.

"I just think it would be foolish to believe we can just hop, skip, and dive headfirst into marriage without giving ourselves time to get to know each other first. It's been what? Six months? We need to see how we react when things aren't all fun and exciting anymore. When shit gets really real, like when we're both having a horrible day and the baby's screaming."

She gazed up into his face. "We deserve to know we can make it through that before we get married."

"So what are you saying?"

"I'm saying, we keep living our lives, loving each other, and you give me some time to catch my breath."

"How much time?"

She shrugged. "As much as I need?"

"I'm a business man, remember? Can I get an estimate?"

Jaylah mulled over an answer until she landed on one that sounded like the truth. "A year. I need a year."

Johnny considered her request for several tense moments.

"And what if I don't want to wait that long?"

She cocked her head and eyeballed him.

"I'm not worth the wait?" Jaylah challenged. "You said you love me and you want to marry me, and we're a family, right? Why would you suddenly change your mind because I need a year?"

Johnny rubbed his temples and let out another gush of air.

"So I don't have a choice in the matter?"

"You always have a choice, Johnny. Even if you don't like the options, you still get to choose."

Jaylah stood and started toward the hotel. When she got to the corner she realized Johnny was still sitting under the clock across from the theater. He appeared to be frozen, or praying, his head bowed and his hands clasped in front of his face.

As she made her way down the avenue Jaylah hoped that whatever Johnny decided wouldn't make her regret her words, which at the moment, had left her all alone.

21

"Still giving me the silent treatment, huh?"

Jaylah watched Johnny slip into his coat and grab his satchel on his way out the door. Since returning from Bordeaux their conversations had been few and far between. Work seemed to once again occupy the majority of Johnny's time, and Jaylah threw herself into the comfortable distraction of deadlines. But a sinking feeling kept nagging at the side of her brain: *Did I fuck this up?*

At first Jaylah was relieved that she'd finally come clean about wanting to postpone the wedding, but as the days rolled by, and their conversations amounted to little more than passing chats about the weather, their schedules, or what they should eat for dinner, she started to get concerned.

New Johnny, the vulnerable man she'd seen in Bordeaux, receded into the background, and Jaylah was left with a brooding lover who appeared too angry to even speak to her.

"Don't start this right now, Jaylah. I've got to get to the office early."

"Right, meetings." She rolled her eyes. "Gotta make that money, right?"

She didn't want to start an argument, but if it got him to show a little passion—to get emotional, or angry, or illustrate that he cared *at all*—she wouldn't mind. Jaylah wanted her Johnny back, but she was afraid she'd pushed him away.

He let out an agitated sigh. "I don't want to fight with you."

"You don't want to do *anything* with me lately, Johnny. What gives?"

He gripped the handle of his bag tighter and glanced at the door. "Look, I'm sorry. I just have a lot to contend with right now."

"Like what?"

He glanced at his watch and sat his bag down.

"Like Femi's in Lagos trying to sure up our deal with Seven Energy and I'm stuck doing twice the work at JPFS, and according to Charles, Fiona's trying to change the terms of our agreement."

Jaylah's eyebrows shot up at the mention of his ex-wife's name. "She what?"

"She's still trying to negotiate, or rather renegotiate. I really don't know what's going on, but Charles says he's handling it." Johnny rubbed the spot where his beard would be if he let it grow, and shrugged. "Sorry I've been a bit preoccupied, but the whole world can't revolve around you, Jaylah."

She recoiled. "What did you say?"

"Nothing. Look, I have to go, okay?"

He turned to leave, but Jaylah rushed to cut him off at the door.

"We're not finished, Johnny," she said, crossing her arms. "Why are you so angry with me?"

He rubbed his eyes and groaned. "I'm not."

"Oh really? You've barely talked to me since we've been back, we haven't made love, and now you're calling me spoiled." She glared at him. "If that's not angry, I don't know what is."

"I can't do this right now, okay? You think I'm angry. Fine. Believe what you want. I'm angry. Now can I leave?"

"It's not about me believing what I want, Johnny. I just want to know what's going on. Every since we agreed to postpone the wedding, things have been—"

Johnny let out a harsh laugh, damn near doubling over as he howled.

"Please...let me in on the joke."

"*We* agreed to postpone the wedding?"

"Yes, we said—"

"*You* said, Jaylah. Not me. Remember that."

She put her hands on her hips. "No, you chose—"

"Let's not even have *that* conversation again. Yes, I chose to agree to your terms. What were alternatives? To breakup? To move out and be a weekend father? To be apart from the woman I love? What kind of fucked up choices did I actually have? You were the one holding all the cards."

"This isn't a game, Johnny. I don't—"

"Damn right it's not a game," he said, raising his voice. "Everything I've done these past few months has been for us, so we can have a good life, and you don't even want it."

Jaylah stepped toward Johnny and grabbed his tie, pulling him in close. She softened her tone.

"I know, and I appreciate everything you do." Jaylah planted a soft kiss on his chin and she could feel him relax. He slid an arm around her waist. "And of course I want this life, babe."

"Just not until next year."

"Johnny, I—"

He kissed her on lips, shushing her. "I get it, Jaylah, okay? I don't like it, but I get it."

As Jaylah watched him walk out the door she hoped he did.

Jourdan waved at Jaylah through the window of Coffee & Candy as soon as she spotted her outside the door. Even though she was in the middle of crafting a pitch to snag her biggest client to date, Jourdan agreed to meet Jaylah for lunch.

"That's what sisters do!" she had said, bushing aside Jaylah's suggestion to just connect later after calling Jourdan in tears.

After her morning conversation with Johnny, Jaylah felt on edge. He said he understood why she wanted to wait a year before getting married, but she wasn't sure he actually did.

When he headed off to work Jaylah fritted around the flat, running their conversation through her head. But after a few hours of thinking of things she *could* have said to make him grasp her point, she realized rehashing the whole thing was pointless and called Jourdan instead.

"You're trying to make me fat, aren't you?" Jaylah said, eyeing the pastries and sweets that lined the walls of the café as she sat down.

"Well, you're five months along, isn't it about time you start looking pregnant?"

"Oh, trust me, I do," she said patting her small bump. "You haven't seen me naked, remember?"

Jourdan chortled. "Perish the thought!"

"How's the pitch coming along?" Jaylah changed the subject wanting to talk about something other than being pregnant. Aside from a serious bout of morning sickness in the beginning, things had moved along without much fuss, and sometimes, Jaylah even forgot she was carrying a child at all.

"Driving me bloody insane!" Jourdan threw up her hand in an exaggerated motion. "I almost want to forget the whole thing."

"You can't do that, J. The 30 Under 30 opening was amazing. Imagine how much of a bigger deal landing the Gagosian account would be for you guys."

Jourdan sipped her Irish coffee. "I know. I just need to get my head in the game."

"Need me to do anything? Who's the competition? I can write something salacious about them." Jaylah laughed, trying to lift her friend's spirits. "They might suddenly find themselves in the middle of a scandal."

"No thanks, sissy. You're supposed to be using your powers for good. I'm the bad twin, remember?"

"Well, the offer's on the table whenever you need it."

"Thanks, Jay." Jourdan patted Jaylah's hand. "Feeling better?"

Jaylah released a long sigh. "Define better?"

"Well, you're offering to take down my competitors and you're not crying anymore, so that's a start."

"Then I guess I am. It's just…" She sat back in her chair and searched for the right words. "I don't want to lose him, Jourdan. He looked so hurt when I came clean about the wedding. And you know how men react when they get hurt."

Jourdan nodded. "They shut down."

"Exactly! And that's what I'm afraid he's doing. We barely talk, we haven't had sex, I don't know what to do."

"It sounds like he needs a little reassurance you don't have one foot out the door."

"I'm pregnant, J, why would I even dream of leaving now?"

"Because you can. And he knows it." Jourdan stirred her coffee. "Look, men like Johnny, men who are used to being the provider and taking care of everyone and everything, they need to feel useful. It probably scares the piss out of him that you don't need him in the way he's used to being needed."

"Because I have a job?"

"And a life, and a career, and your own flat—which he's probably not really happy he lives in, by the way."

"He's never said anything about that..."

"Why would he, Jay? He wants to be with you, and the last time he mentioned getting a place together you shut him down."

Jaylah shook her head. "But that was back when I wasn't even sure I was keeping the baby."

"And? Men have long memories, too," Jourdan said. "Think about it. Johnny can buy just about any house in London, but he's sharing a one bedroom flat you subleased from someone else. Where are you guys going to put the baby? In the pantry?" Jourdan laughed at her own suggestion. "He's a planner, Jay. You don't think he made all that money by accident, do you?"

Jaylah stared at Jourdan unable to speak, bowled over by her friend's insight.

Had Johnny been following her lead all along? Did she *really* hold all the cards like he said she did?

Jourdan continued, snatching Jaylah out of her thoughts.

"And all of his plans are being derailed by the woman he loves most who happens to needs him the least. Johnny probably doesn't even know how to handle it all."

Jaylah considered her friend's words. Was Johnny going through the motions and agreeing to *all* of her terms just to make her happy? Did he want something more, but was afraid to voice his own needs because he didn't want to lose *her?*

"Oh my God, J! You're right. He's been settling...for me," she said, bringing a hand to her chest like she had a breakthrough.

Jourdan nodded at Jaylah, looking pleased.

"And all this time I thought I was the one bending over backward for him..."

Jaylah couldn't believe it. While she spent months considering what *she* needed from the relationship to feel comfortable, loved, and respected, she never gave Johnny's needs the same amount of contemplation.

Because of their beginning, things *had* to be on her terms, right? How else could she be certain he wouldn't run off and fall in love with the next woman who made him feel alive?

But while Jaylah was busy guarding her heart, trying to read between Johnny's words, testing the limits of his patience, and doling out her trust in tiny increments, she couldn't see what was right in front of her eyes. Johnny had given himself to her fully, completely, and without reservation. And she was the one who was holding back.

Jaylah shot out of her seat and threw on her coat.

"I gotta go"

"What? Where? We haven't even eaten yet."

"I know, J. But I *have* to go see him. We need to sort this out!" Jaylah rushed to the other side of the table and kissed her friend on the cheek. "Thanks Jourdan...for everything."

"No problem, sissy. It's my pleasure."

Jaylah pulled £20 out of her purse and laid it on the table.

"Lunch is on me," she said before running out café to get her man.

Jaylah bounded off the elevator and into the office of JPFS just as the receptionist was leaving to take a late lunch.

"Hey, is Mr. Poku in a meeting?" she asked as the woman stepped past her and onto the lift.

"No, but he's..."

The doors closed before the receptionist had a chance to finish her sentence. Jaylah checked herself out in the plate glass window overlooking the wharf, smoothing down stray hairs and wishing she had gone home to change into something a little sexier than jeans and a flowery tunic before surprising Johnny.

After deciding she looked presentable enough, Jaylah rushed down the hall toward Johnny's office with a sudden gleeful bounce in her step.

We're going to fix this. We're going to get back to our normal life, she thought as she reached his office.

Jaylah rapped on the door with two quick knocks and plastered a huge smile on her face. Instead of waiting for Johnny to welcome her in she opened the door, but stopped in her tracks when she saw a raven-haired woman sitting across from him.

Johnny glanced up from behind his desk and looked startled to see her in the doorway.

"Jaylah? What are you doing here?"

"Oh, I'm sorry," she stammered. "Your receptionist said you weren't in a meeting. I'll just wait in the—"

The woman turned to look at Jaylah bringing her sentence to an abrupt halt. Something flickered in the woman's eyes making Jaylah feel uneasy about the scene. Immediately, her heart picked up its beat and every nerve in her body stood on end.

"It's okay, Jaylah. This is—"

"Fiona," Jaylah whispered like she'd conjured up a ghost.

She stumbled backward, resting against the large oak door. Jaylah felt light-headed and fought off the urge to faint—or kick Fiona's ass for daring to show up at *her* man's office—but she waited to see what would happen next.

"Jaylah?" Johnny stood and began moving around his desk.

She steadied herself and held up a hand. "I'm good."

Johnny sat back down, but eyed Jaylah carefully, worry creasing his face.

"Fiona was just about to leave."

A smirk crossed her red lips. "Yes, I'm on my way out. Pleasure meeting you."

Fiona stood, walked toward Jaylah and extended her hand. As she got closer Jaylah noticed the outline of her protruding belly pushing against the fabric of her shift dress.

"You're pregnant?" Jaylah asked, ignoring Fiona's polite gesture.

"Yes," she smiled, rubbing her belly in that sickening sweet way exuberant mothers do. "I'm six months along."

"Six months..." Jaylah repeated, stunned.

Fiona glanced at Johnny and grinned. "I hear you are, too. I guess congratulations are in order?"

Jaylah looked from Johnny to Fiona wondering what the fuck was happening. Why was she in his office? Why did she know her business? And more importantly, who was the father of her child?

That last question knocked all of the fight out of Jaylah. Watching her fiancé interact with his *pregnant* ex-wife made her feel like the walls of Johnny's office were closing in. Jaylah had to get out of there. She couldn't deal with what Fiona's revelation possibly meant to her life.

Six months.

Jaylah turned on her heels and hurried down the corridor. She repeatedly punched the button for the elevator, hoping it would get to her before Johnny, *or Fiona,* saw her tears.

"Jaylah..." Johnny said, moving swiftly to catch up with her. "Jaylah wait...wait!"

The doors opened just in time and Jaylah jumped on the lift, escaping the horror she found at JPFS. When she reached the ground floor her phone began to ring. Johnny. She pressed ignore and took off running through the courtyard to the nearest subway station, just in case he was able to fly down 27 flights of stairs to find her.

Jaylah's phone rang all the way to Canary Wharf station. She ignored all of Johnny's calls and descended the stairs of the Tube in a daze. She paced the platform replaying the drama of last few minutes.

Until now, Jaylah had been unable to put a face to the boogeyman, but after seeing Fiona—poised, porcelain-skinned, stunning Fiona—Jaylah suddenly felt like she couldn't compete.

Fiona was everything she was not. Jaylah was attractive but she wasn't polished or sophisticated in the same way Fiona seemed to be. And while Johnny loved her fiercely, his family, and especially his father, loved Fiona.

What if the Poku clan never accepted Jaylah and her child? Would Johnny continue to stand by her side, or would he grow to resent giving up his family for her?

Jaylah felt antsy. She couldn't go home, Johnny was likely already in a cab heading toward their flat, and she couldn't call Jourdan and beg her friend to take another break from her project to rescue her *again.*

When the train finally arrived Jaylah knew where she could go to find a sympathetic ear and someone who would make sure she was okay.

22

Jaylah stood in front of the ornate door trying to convince herself to go home, or to the Tate, or anywhere but Faraj's flat. At that moment she felt broken in a way only Johnny would understand, but she could not bear seeing him, too afraid he might confirm the fear mounting in her body.

This can't be happening. He can't be the father of Fiona's baby, her brain screamed.

The timing made it possible. Six months ago he still shared their marital home, still probably slept in their bed, still was her husband. Even though Johnny claimed he hadn't had been with Fiona since his and Jaylah's first date, how could she be sure?

A new sense of anger rose up in Jaylah. If Johnny had lied to her, if he had fathered Fiona's child, it was over. They were finished; there was no coming back from two babies by two women only a month apart.

How could she stick around if he'd played her for the fool *again?*

Jaylah knocked on Faraj's door in need of a little ego stroking, and possibly some revenge. The way she was feeling, either one would do. After a few minutes, she heard him bounding down the stairs and Jaylah tried to erase any evidence of hurt from her eyes. She manufactured a smile and waited for Faraj to open the door.

The look on his face said it all; he was surprised to see her.

"Jaylah? What are you doing here?"

"I was in the neighborhood and I thought I would drop by. I didn't catch you at a bad time, did I?"

"No, no. Not at all. I was just working on a painting."

"Oh. I don't want to wreck your flow. I'll catch you another time then."

Jaylah turned to leave, slightly relieved he was already preoccupied and she wouldn't make a fool of herself, or do something reckless.

Faraj caught her by the hand.

"No, please stay." He smiled so brightly Jaylah was briefly dazed. "I always feel more inspired when I see you. Come on up."

She followed him up the stairs, trying to keep her eyes off his perfect ass. Faraj was built like a light heavyweight boxer with muscular arms, tight abs, and a strong, capable back. Months ago, after making out in the back of a cab on the way to her place, Jaylah had felt like she'd won a prize when he shed his clothes and exposed his defined physique.

They reached his living room and Jaylah gravitated toward the photographs lining Faraj's mantelpiece again, looking at each one as if she was seeing them for the first time.

"Can I take your coat?" he asked, standing behind her.

Jaylah swallowed hard, aware of how close they were to actually touching.

"Sure"

He slipped off her coat, letting his fingers trace the tops of her arms as he removed it. Instead of putting it away, he took a step closer and gently brushed her hair aside.

"You have a lovely neck, Jaylah," he whispered. "Perfect for..."

She whipped around to face him, hoping to stop whatever was about to happen from happening.

"Thanks!"

Faraj smirked. "Can I get you something to drink?"

"A glass of wine would be great," she said, feeling on edge.

Jaylah had gone to Faraj's looking to take her mind off the scene in Johnny's office, but as she stood in the middle of his flat, Jaylah wondered if she had made a terrible mistake. Sure getting back at Johnny would feel good in the short term, but was she really ready to do something impetuous and throw away her future before she even had all the answers?

"I hope you don't mind red."

Faraj handed her a glass, temporarily quieting the doubt and confusion growing in her mind. Jaylah took a large swig of the wine and waited for the familiar lightheadedness to set in.

He watched her gulp the merlot. "Long day?"

She took another generous swallow. "You could say that."

"Want to talk about it?"

"Not if we can help it." Jaylah offered a weak smile, needing to change the subject before saying something she couldn't take back. "What were you working on when I popped up unannounced?"

"I'll show you." He offered his hand, and after a few seconds of deliberation, she took it.

Faraj led the way, stepping aside for Jaylah to enter once they reached his painting room. Like last time, the walls were covered in sketches and a canvas sat on an easel in the middle of it all. This time, however, the canvas wasn't empty; it held the beginnings of a woman's face.

He led her to a chair in the corner of the room near the window.

"Sit here."

Jaylah plopped down, feeling the soothing buzz of the wine. Faraj returned to the easel and started sketching.

She watched him for a few seconds before realizing what was happening.

"Are you drawing me?"

He continued drafting, stealing glances in her direction while his hand moved across the canvas.

"Umm hmm."

"No, no, no, no, no. You can't draw me. I'm covering you remember? I can't be a part of any exhibition. How would that look?"

"This isn't for the public. It's a gift."

She cocked her head to the side. "A gift?"

"Perfect, keep your head just like that," Faraj said, his hand feverishly working over the taut fabric.

"What kind of a gift, Faraj?"

"To go with the other one."

She stared at him, perplexed. "What other one? What are you talking about?"

He continued outlining her features, adding details and using his finger to shade lines.

"The one I sent you this afternoon. Didn't you get it?"

She thought back over her chaotic day and shivered. "No. I've been out all afternoon. What is it?"

"I sent you the other painting. The one from the gallery exhibit."

Jaylah gasped. "Of the woman?"

He smiled, but kept working. "Of you."

She was stunned. Jaylah was drawn to the painting at the opening because it felt sensual and powerful in a familiar way, but it was also expensive. Faraj could have easily netted thirty or forty thousand pounds for it if he wanted, but he had given it to her instead. Could she accept such an extravagant gift from a man she'd been intimate with?

What would Johnny think

The thought shot through her brain without warning, making her feel uncomfortable.

Jaylah quickly drained her glass of wine. She wanted to forget about Johnny for a while. She couldn't stomach the possibility of her life crumbling in such a spectacular way: pregnant by her married fiancé who had possibly also knocked up his ex-wife. The whole thing sounded like a tragic episode of Jerry Springer and Jaylah couldn't believe she'd gotten herself into such a fucked up predicament again.

"Can I have another glass of wine?"

Faraj added a few more touches to the sketch. "Sure, love."

When he left the room Jaylah checked her phone: 14 messages. She scrolled through the texts from Johnny, each asking where she was and why she wasn't answering the phone. She hit delete, erasing them en masse, but paused when she spotted one from Jourdan. "Johnny called looking for you. Everything alright, sissy???!"

Jaylah wondered what Johnny was thinking. He must have been going out of his mind if he called Jourdan to locate her. The way she bolted out of his office, Jaylah figured he was afraid she was going to leave him, or jump off Tower Bridge. The idea caused a self-satisfied grin to dance across her face.

Serves him right, she thought before replying to Jourdan.

"I'm fine, J. Just clearing my head. Will explain later. Love you."

Jaylah turned off her phone and slipped it back in her purse.

Faraj returned with her merlot and a suspicious look on his face. "Here you go."

She took a gulp and smiled.

"You know, you can tell me about it right?"

"Tell you about what?" she asked, trying to ignore his concern.

"Whatever's troubling you. Don't pretend like it's nothing, Jaylah."

She shrugged and took another sip. "Shouldn't you get back to sketching?"

He shook his head and a smirked. "Now you want me to paint you? You don't have to hide from me, you know."

Yes, I do, she shot back in her mind, but didn't utter a word.

He crouched down in front of her and Jaylah's face began to feel warm. "Tell me what's bothering you, love. Please?"

Jaylah stared into his dark, glimmering eyes trying to decide what to do. It would be easy to confide in Faraj and unleash the storm of emotions brewing in her belly. But if she told him the whole sordid tale about her and Johnny and Fiona, Jaylah was afraid Faraj would look at her differently, or worse, try to save her.

She put a hand to the side of his face and traced his stubble with her fingertips.

"It's a long, long story."

"I have time."

She outlined his full lips with her index finger. "And it's not pretty."

He kissed her palm. "That's okay. Mine aren't either."

Jaylah draped her arms around Faraj's neck. "It's about me and a man."

He nodded. "Figured as much."

"This man..." she hesitated, "he might be having a baby with someone else, and..."

He put his hand over her heart. "It hurts right here."

"Yes," Jaylah whispered, trying to dam her tears before they hit her cheeks.

Faraj leaned forward and kissed the spot where his hand had been. "All better?"

She chuckled. "I wish."

He skimmed his lips across her neck, then hovered over her mouth. "Better?"

Jaylah shook her head.

Faraj kissed one cheek and then the other. "How about now?"

Jaylah held her breath and tried to quell the craving snaking up her thighs. Faraj was not only incredibly handsome, but he was also achingly tender, only going as far as she would allow.

He found her forehead with his lips. "Any better?"

Jaylah released a lusty sigh. "A little."

It had been weeks since Bordeaux, weeks since Johnny covered her body with his, and she yearned for his touch. Jaylah wanted to be back in her flat making love to her man like they did before things got so complicated and hard, but Faraj was right here, offering himself up like an exquisite gift. How could she turn him away?

He met her gaze and stared into her eyes; Jaylah trembled with nervous excitement when she saw desire flash across his face.

"Tell me what I can do to make you feel better, Jaylah," Faraj whispered. "Tell me, please."

His hands caressed her face like it was a delicate piece of art. Faraj's breathing slowed and deepened, and his hunger for Jaylah was palpable. His eyes bore into hers, but he held back, waiting for permission.

Jaylah knew she could make love to him if she wanted. She knew he would consider it his duty to please her in every way possible. And she knew she would enjoy it.

But was she ready to jeopardize what she loved most for a few hours of relief?

"Kiss me," Jaylah said before she could take back the words.

Faraj moved swiftly, pulling her closer and nibbling her bottom lip before kissing both of them. His tongue played against hers and his hands found their way into her thick mass of curls.

Jaylah was spinning out of control. Her mind told her to push him away, grab her coat, and run out the door, but her body rebelled, delighting in Faraj's touch, which ignited the pent-up yearning that had been building for weeks. Jaylah wanted so, so badly to give in.

Faraj pulled back and looked at her.

"What?" she asked, breathless.

"Just admiring you. You're such a stunning woman, Jaylah, and you don't even seem to know it."

She felt awkward and exposed under his intense gaze, which seemed to look past her reserved façade to catch a glimpse of who she was on the inside--ardent, wanton, and fiery.

Faraj found her lips again and slid his hand under her tunic, inching it up her torso until he slipped it over her head and let it fall to the floor. He palmed her breasts, moving his mouth to her neck, sucking her skin gently.

A dull ache throbbed in her core, and Jaylah arched her back as Faraj slid a bra strap over her shoulder, pressing his lips against the indentation it left in her skin. She ran her fingers through his hair and slung her arms around his neck, content to let him do all the work. After all, she needed pleasing and Faraj seemed more than willing to oblige.

Fireworks exploded in Jaylah's body when he slipped a hand inside her bra and began squeezing one of her nipples.

"I never stopped thinking of you, Jaylah. Not once, love," he murmured between heavy breaths into her hair.

She exhaled a moan and he took her sighs as confirmation she was ready for more. Faraj reached for her waistband and unbuckled her jeans. He slid his hand inside, brushing against her stomach to get to the space between her thighs. Jaylah flinched like she'd been burned by his touch and quickly pushed him away.

He gaped at her, confused. "What is it?"

"I...I have to go," she stuttered, standing too quickly, her head swimming and dizzy. "I can't do this."

"I don't understand. Did I do something wrong?"

"No you didn't." She grabbed her blouse and picked up her bag. "It's me. I...I'm...I can't do this to him, Faraj."

"Is this about the article?" he asked, watching her shimmy into her tunic. "Fuck the article. I want you more than being in a magazine, Jaylah."

Faraj tried to grab her hand, but she fled to the other room.

Jaylah bounced around the parlor like pinball, searching for her coat and apologizing for her hasty exodus. Faraj was sexy and available and sweet, but he wasn't Johnny. And when his hand touched her belly she was reminded of where she needed to be—sorting out her relationship, not running blindly into Faraj's arms looking for an escape.

She mumbled to herself as she put on her boots, wondering how she almost let it all slip through her hands.

"I was so close to...I can't believe I almost...my God."

Faraj trailed behind her trying to figure out what was going on. Jaylah told herself she would explain it all later. She would send him an email or a letter, or maybe when she and Johnny were on solid footing, she would see him again. But at that moment all Jaylah knew was she needed to get out of there—fast.

She found her coat and threw it over her shoulders, moving toward the stairs.

"Jaylah, please don't leave like this. I don't know what happened, but we can—"

She cut him off. "Faraj, I'm so sorry. My head is all over the place and I shouldn't have come. I'm sorry, I really am, but I need to go now." Jaylah turned to head toward the exit. "I've got enough information for the article, so I'll just write it up and send it to my editor. Please don't call me, okay Faraj? I just need some ti—"

Jaylah missed the top step, too busy explaining and hurrying and apologizing to notice how close she was to Faraj's staircase.

When she realized she was going to fall, Jaylah tried to grab the banister and steady herself, but it was too late. She tumbled to the floor, landing facedown with an audible thud.

Faraj rushed to her side, alarmed by the trickle of blood coming from her head.

"Jaylah?" he called gently while she lay on the ground. "Jaylah can you hear me? Jaylah?" When Faraj noticed she wasn't moving he raced upstairs to call an ambulance.

Jaylah could hear him pacing in the living room above, voice raised and frantic giving the dispatcher his address.

Okay Jay, get up. We need to get home. C'mon, get up...

Jaylah's head pounded, her wrists were sore from trying to break her fall, and her back felt like she was lying on a bed of scalding nails, every nerve burning and raw. Jaylah gathered her strength and struggled to her feet, still intent on and heading home. But after taking a step, she collapsed on the steps, overcome by an excruciating spasm.

"Jaylah?" Faraj ran down and sat next to her. "Don't move. The ambulance service is on the way, okay? Don't try to move. Everything will be fine, yeah?"

Faraj used his shirt to wipe blood off her forehead just as another stabbing pain reverberated from her back and across her belly. She doubled over, instinctively cradling her stomach hoping to protect her baby.

"Oh my God....oh my God...my baby..." Jaylah mouthed over and over again, afraid of what the fall might have done to her child. "Please God. Please, please, please."

Jaylah tried not to get hysterical, but as she sat hunched against the wall in anguish, she could no longer hold back her tears. She cried for the pain winding its way through her body; she cried because she was terrified of losing the baby; and she cried because the one person she wanted and needed most was not the man sitting next to her.

23

Jaylah drifted in and out of consciousness while she lay in bed at King's College Hospital, catching bits and pieces of the conversation going on around her. The last thing she remembered was being strapped to a gurney and zipping through the halls on the way to an observation room. The pain shooting through her body had caused her to pass out, and when she came to, they were loading her into a MRI machine.

Snatches of memories floated through her head. Running out of Johnny's office, kissing Faraj, the fall, the ambulance ride, the look on his face when she told him not to accompany her to the hospital.

"I can't let you go alone," Faraj had said, stroking her hand. He'd jumped in the back of the coach before they were about to pull off, but Jaylah stopped them from whisking him along for the ride.

"I won't be alone," she struggled to say, as they hooked her up to the monitors. "They'll call Johnny...my fiancé. He'll take care of me. It's going to be fine, okay, Faraj? I'm sorry...about everything."

Faraj had slunk away like a rejected puppy, but Jaylah knew it was best. Though she didn't mean to hurt his feelings, she and Johnny had enough drama to resolve without adding her afternoon in his flat to the mix.

Jaylah opened her eyes and saw Johnny sitting in a chair next to her bed, praying. His clothes were disheveled, his eyes were shut tight, and she could hear him begging God for her safety. She watched him wipe away a few escaped tears from his cheeks, and her heart broke.

Jaylah wanted their relationship to survive both their indiscretions, but his seemed far too big to ignore.

After searching for every possible reason not to have the baby, not to remain tied to the man she feared would be her undoing because she loved him just that much, Jaylah would've been gutted if she lost him or their little one now.

She gasped.

The baby...

Jaylah's hands flew to her tiny bump, hoping it provided enough cushion during her tumble down the stairs. Because she was obsessed with surfing baby blogs and forums, Jaylah had read countless stories of women tripping on patches of ice or getting into minor car accidents and losing their babies. So, she was terrified that her belly flop down more than a dozen stairs spelled utter disaster for little Nemo.

She began bargaining with God to let her baby arrive safely.

"God, I know I don't talk to you enough, but this isn't about me," she said quietly. "This child *deserves* to be loved the way we can love it. And I know I've been stubborn...about all of it...but please, God, please, let my baby make it into the world." Her voice cracked, "Please..."

Johnny's eyes shot open and he sprang to his feet at the sound of her sobbing.

"Jaylah? What is it? Need me to get the doctor?"

He was halfway to the door when she stopped him, yelling his name. He returned to her side and gently caressed her hand.

"Are you alright, Jay?"

She nodded. "I'm okay." Jaylah tried to sit up, to prove she was fine, but a sharp pain pierced her back, causing her to yelp.

"Don't move, babes. You bruised your tailbone in the fall. You have to stay still."

She grimaced until the sharp jab subsided.

"When can I get up and move around?"

"Later today if you're feeling up to it, but you'll have to take it very slow. The doctor said for the next two days we've got to ice you down and keep you as comfortable as possible."

Later today?

Jaylah glanced out the window and saw the sun peeking through the clouds. She had been rushed to the hospital in the late afternoon, how could it possibly still be daylight?

"What time is it?" she asked, trying to get her bearings straight.

"Just after seven."

"In the morning?"

"Yes. You've been here since yesterday."

Jaylah looked at Johnny's wrinkled shirt, its sleeves were rolled up past his elbows and it was open at the neck.

"So have you?"

"I came as soon as they called and I'm not leaving here without you."

Tears flooded her eyes; Johnny's commitment was astounding, and for the first time Jaylah wondered if she deserved it. She was so close to throwing away everything they had because seeing Fiona made her doubt herself, and them.

But there was no denying Johnny loved her and was hell bent on staying by Jaylah's side, even when she tried her hardest to run away.

Jaylah noticed her left wrist was bandaged and she held it up to Johnny.

"Sprained." He released a thick sigh and rubbed his eyes. "Thankfully nothing is broken."

"And..." Jaylah was afraid to ask about Nemo, too scared Johnny would tell her they'd lost their child because she had been so careless. "...the baby?"

Johnny smiled for the first time. "He's perfectly fine."

"He?" Jaylah asked, the news of their baby's gender catching her by surprise.

"Yeah, we're having a boy!"

He kissed her forehead and she beamed. "More Pokus to carry on the bloodline, eh?"

Johnny laughed, the tension seeming to melt from his shoulders, which were back to being proud and upright just like Jaylah liked them.

He pounded his chest. "Damn straight."

They were quiet for several minutes, the news of their baby's safety giving them both something to be thankful for. Jaylah put her hand to her belly and Johnny covered it with his.

He met her eyes. "You didn't try to..."

"No, it was an accident. I wouldn't dare do something like this on purpose. I may be a little crazy and hormonal, but I haven't lost my mind."

Johnny exhaled. "I'm sorry, babes. When you ran out the office and wouldn't answer your phone I didn't know what to think."

"I should be the one apologizing. After I saw Fiona, and her belly, I was thrown for a loop. Look, whatever happened—"

"It's not my child, Jaylah."

"What?"

"You ran out before I could explain. Fiona's baby isn't mine, Jay."

She searched his eyes for a flinch, or an averted gaze, or a tell, but found none. Even if Johnny wasn't lying, there could still be a chance, right? Jaylah was afraid to get her hopes up.

"How can you be sure? The timing—"

"Doesn't fit. At all," he assured her.

"But you guys were still—"

He cut her off again. "We weren't."

"Are you sure?"

"Positive." He kissed her lips, but Jaylah couldn't just let it go.

"But does she think you are? Is that why she was at your office?" Jaylah wanted, no needed, *all* the answers; she couldn't abide any more secrets between them. "I can't have her popping up again, Johnny. We've been through so much already, I don't want anything else coming between us."

"I know, babes. But no, that's not why she was there. She doesn't want to keep the house. She wants to sell it and move to another flat. She just wanted to be sure she could keep the profits from the transaction."

"And you don't mind?"

"Why should I? We don't need it." He kissed the back of Jaylah's hand. "But as far as the baby goes, turns out she met some Scottish bloke during holiday and well, " he shrugged, "before we even consummated our relationship they were already having a fling."

Jaylah gasped. "You mean...she cheated on *you?* I'm not a home wrecker?"

"You were *never* a home wrecker, Jaylah, I told you that."

"I've been wracking my brain and blaming myself for breaking up your marriage and getting pregnant and all this time..." her voice trailed off.

Jaylah thought back over all the months she wasted feeling guilty about loving Johnny and trying to purposely push him away in the hopes he'd go careening back to his wife and her karma wouldn't be fucked up forever. It was true, she loved him fiercely, but Jaylah hated herself for ruining Fiona's happy home.

"Wow, all this time..."

Jaylah couldn't believe she'd ever considered walking away from Johnny, from being loved so completely she barely knew how to handle it. He made her feel safe and cared for and beautiful. And Jaylah knew he would stand by her through good times and bad, slaying any dragon that dared to rear its ugly head.

The way Johnny loved her felt overwhelming and magnificent all at once, and sometimes, Jaylah wondered if he could say the same.

"Babe? I went to your office because I wanted to tell you something."

He pushed the hair away from her face and sat on the edge of her bed.

"What's that?"

"These past few weeks things have been...not so good."

He kissed her forehead. "I know, my ego got the better of me, babes. But I understand why you want to wait to get married, and after yesterday, that's not even the most important thing anymore. I just want to make sure you and our son are fine."

"Me too, which is why I think we should start looking for a house."

Johnny's eyes lit up and a huge smile crossed his face. "Are you sure?"

"We're a family, right?"

He nodded.

"So, our family needs a home. And another thing..." Jaylah kissed his chin, loving the feel of stubble against her lips. "Every decision that needs to be made from now on, we'll make it together, okay?"

"Looks like you should've bumped your head sooner," he said, chuckling. "But seriously, where is this coming from?"

"You were right, Johnny. I *was* holding all the cards. But if things are going to work between us, I can't make all the rules. We have to create them together."

Johnny nuzzled her nose, then planted a tender kiss on her lips. Jaylah was tired of fighting what felt natural; she loved Johnny and she was sick of trying to justify how, or why, it all happened so quickly. From this moment on, she promised herself she was just going to enjoy it.

Jaylah pulled Johnny closer, parting his mouth with her tongue before planting warm kisses all over face and neck.

"Oh this is just bloody sick!" a voice said from the doorway. Jaylah and Johnny looked up to find Jourdan standing in the threshold pretending to gag. "Glad to see you're alive, sissy."

Jourdan walked to Jaylah's bedside, kissed her friend on the cheek, and then waved at Johnny.

"So I'm guessing Nemo's fine? When Johnny told me what happened, I was so worried..." Jourdan's eyes welled up.

Jaylah patted her best friend's hand. "Your nephew is perfectly fine, J. Swimming along as usual."

"Nephew?!" Jourdan shouted. "Ohmygod, Jay! We're having a boy!"

Jourdan hugged her sister, and although she was still in pain, Jaylah was happy to be surrounded by two of her favorite people in the world. It had taken more than 28 years, but she had finally found her tribe.

Flanked by her fiancé and her sister, Jaylah knew whatever happened next, whatever crazy twist that came her way, Johnny and Jourdan would be right there by her side.

Jaylah said a silent prayer of thanks for her family, because without them, she would have never discovered how wonderful her life could be.

"Oh bloody hell, Jay, you know what I realized?"

"What's that?"

"Nemo's a boy!" Jourdan shook her head and chortled. "Just what the world needs, another dick!"

About the Author

Britni Danielle is a Los Angeles-based freelance writer whose work has appeared in numerous publications including *Essence, Jet, Ebony.com, Clutch, and Vibe.*

Enjoyed reading *Two Steps Back*? Please leave a review, and tell Britni what you thought of the book on Twitter @BritniDWrites or on her blog, BritniDanielle.com.

Made in the USA
Lexington, KY
21 June 2014